P

"Just fini... Loved it!! Defini... can't wait to post my 5 star review! Thanks for giving me a chance to read this early. Loved the Peggy & Steve cameo. Always nice to see old friends." ~ **Sherry Troop**

"With a visit from garden mystery series hostess, Peggy Lee, this new series is off to a good start when Sarah Tucker arrives to sell the abandoned property she once loved as a child only to find mystery, romance, and a surprise or two. Will she stay and follow in her grandparents' footsteps or follow her parents' lead? A worthy successor to the Lavene's writing lineup!" ~ **Joan Black, Writing World**.

"(Killing Weeds, Peggy Lee Garden Mystery) was a wonderfully written story with plenty of mystery coming from every direction. There was never a dull moment. I turned each page eagerly awaiting what would come next. The Lavenes have taken the twists and turns associated with mystery and supersized them. When the reveal came, I was completely shocked! Check out the back of the book for Peggy Lee's Garden Journal, a yummy recipe, and gardening tips for keeping our bee friends happy."
~ **Lisa K's Book Reviews**

Praise for the Peggy Lee Garden Mysteries:

"A Fantastic amateur sleuth." ~ The Best Reviews

"I love the world of Peggy Lee!" ~ Fresh Fiction

Some of our other series:

Peggy Lee Garden Mysteries
Pretty Poison
Fruit of the Poisoned Tree
Poisoned Petals
Perfect Poison
A Corpse For Yew
Buried by Buttercups—Novella
A Thyme to Die
Lethal Lilly
Killing Weeds

Renaissance Faire Mysteries
Wicked Weaves
Ghastly Glass
Deadly Daggers
Harrowing Hats
Treacherous Toy
Perilous Pranks—Novella
Murderous Matrimony
Bewitching Boots

Missing Pieces Mysteries
A Timely Vision
A Touch of Gold
A Spirited Gift
A Haunting Dream
A Finder's Fee
Dae's Christmas Past
A Watery Death

Give 'Em Pumpkin to Talk About

By

Joyce and Jim Lavene

Book coach and editor—Jeni Chappelle
http://www.jenichappelle.com/

Chapter One

"Who are you?" Her heart pounded as she struggled to get the small handgun out of her purse after he'd popped up from the tall grass. "What are you doing here?"

"Whoa." He held up his hands. "You aren't from around here, are you?"

"I'm actually from right here. Not that it has anything to do with you. I'm calling the sheriff."

He leaned closer, his eyes locking with hers. He still held his hands at shoulder height. "Sarah? Is that you?"

"I'm the one asking the questions." She shook the gun at him. This was the only time she'd held the weapon since she'd taken lessons to get her license. "You haven't answered yet—who are you, and why are you on my property?"

The conversation was made more difficult by the tall man in ragged jeans and flannel shirt grinning at her the whole time. If he was afraid, she couldn't tell it. She'd shaken the gun at him thinking he might not have noticed it. People in Misty River tended to use shotguns and rifles. Her miniscule handgun probably wasn't very impressive.

"Well." He squinted, looking away from her toward the tall grass that seemed to grow everywhere on the old farm. "I live here. My name is Jack. And you should never pull a gun on someone unless you're going to use it."

Sarah yelped as he snatched the gun from her, emptied the bullets, and then handed it back.

"Bad things could happen," he continued.

"Well obviously I'd planned to use it," she argued. "Get off my land."

He smiled, showing even white teeth in the midst of an overwhelming brown beard that seemed to cover everything on his face but his cheerful, blue eyes. "No one else from the family has been here for sixteen years. What made you show up all of a sudden?"

She wished she still had the option of pulling out the gun. Now she was at a disadvantage.

"That's none of your business. Just leave before you go to jail."

His interested gaze scanned her from head to toe. She could imagine that he was even more amused by her threats as she stood there in her polite, navy blue suit and heels, her straight, shoulder-length blond hair full of seeds and nettles from the grass and weeds.

"Not to brag," he said with a smile. "But it would take a lot more than you and the sheriff to get rid of me."

Sarah didn't know what else to say and thought of retreating back through the tall grass to get away from him. She couldn't hope to throw him off the property by herself, but his bragging about no one being able to send him away made her angry.

"Sarah?" Her friend, Hunter, yelled from the front of the house where her car was parked. "Are you out there?"

"I'm here," she shouted. When she looked back, the raggedy man was gone. Had she imagined him? No. The bullets he'd emptied from her gun were still on the ground. "Just a minute. I'm headed your way."

She crouched to pick them up and didn't waste any time getting back to what seemed like civilization—the front of the property where the grass had been cut. She snagged her jacket, and probably ruined her heels, as she sprinted through the weeds.

Hunter Ollson was waiting for her, a hand at her forehead trying to shade her deep blue eyes from the sun. "I didn't realize you wanted to walk the property. I would've come with you. It's kind of wild, isn't it?"

"It's been a long time. I didn't expect it to be landscaped but not this bad either. And I didn't plan to walk out there—it just kind of happened."

How could Sarah explain the excitement that had welled up in her when she'd pulled up to the house? It had been like being a child again. The last time she'd been here was when she was twelve—the day her grandparents had vanished.

It was a long story that seemed like ancient history and one she didn't want to burden Hunter with. She had been glad that her friend from college was willing to come to Misty River with her to check on the property. Hunter had been in Richmond on business when Sarah's mother had asked her to take care of the abandoned farm.

"Wow! How big is this anyway?" Hunter asked.

"A hundred and eighty acres." Sarah looked up at the old white, two-story house that needed painting. There were places on the roof where the shingles were missing and a few of the stairs on the porch looked bad. But it was still as beautiful and special as it had been to her as a child.

Her mother had been born here. Sarah had spent every moment she could from the time she could first remember helping with the pumpkin patch, the corn shucking, and bean picking. She'd known the place by heart from the river to the cornfields and the old stone well. She'd helped her grandfather repair the old tree swing and the tractor. They'd picked cucumbers and baled hay.

The sign that said *Misty River Pumpkin Patch* was barely hanging by a single chain at the front of the drive. Other parts of the property—the barn, corn silo, and garage where the tractor was kept—were in bad shape too. The walls were collapsing, and one of the roofs had holes in it.

But what wonderful memories she had of growing up here. Even the dismal, real-life appearance of the property couldn't stop her from eagerly walking out on the land she once loved so well. She could almost believe she was running to greet her grandparents again. How she wished it were true.

"I can't believe your family just wants to get rid of the place." Hunter's blond hair was almost white in the strong September sunshine. She was six-feet tall, statuesque rather than thin, and as beautiful as a model. "I wish my family had a farm like this. It would be great for the weekends. You still seem to like the old place. Why not keep it?"

Realizing they'd reached the part where she'd have to explain what had happened here that had soured her family and left a pall on the land for them, Sarah was glad to see her real estate agent roll up in a *Nash Realty* pickup.

Mace Nash lived locally and had seemed the perfect person to sell the land for Sarah, her mother, and brother. Sarah shook his hand and introduced herself.

Mr. Nash's narrow, brown eyes passed between her and Hunter in appreciation. "Two pretty young blonds! Somebody's looking out for me today! Welcome to Misty River."

He shook hands with Hunter, lingering over her touch, and then seemed to remember that he was there to do business.

"I have the papers ready." He laid them out on the hood of his red pickup for her to sign. "The land is worth some money. Probably ten or fifteen thousand per acre. No one wants to restore the old place. Too bad. I always brought my kids here in the fall for the pumpkins and the ride in the hay wagon. Your grandparents were good people."

Sarah didn't want to talk about it as she signed the documents to allow Nash Realty to represent her in the sale of the property. She didn't belong here anymore. She had a life in Richmond working as an attorney for a Virginia state senator.

"You ever hear from them?" he asked. "Or figure out what happened? People still wonder."

"No." Sarah wished she didn't have to talk about it. Thinking about it was hard enough.

Her grandparents had disappeared one night in late August. Her mother had brought her out to see them on the busiest weekend of the year—the start of pumpkin season. But they'd been gone. The kitchen table had been set. The plates had beans and potatoes on them as though they were about to sit down and eat. There'd still been a cast-iron skillet with cornbread in it on the stove. But no sign of her grandparents.

Later she'd learned from her mother that the sheriff had investigated. There was no blood. No signs of foul play. It was as though someone or something had just lifted them up and carried them away.

Hunter didn't say anything about Sarah's grandparents, but she knew she'd heard Mr. Nash's remark.

"People were real surprised to see someone from the family come back to town." He looked at her signature on the three documents and then handed her one of the copies. "We thought someone else might pay the back taxes and buy the place. I guess your mother wasn't interested in it, huh?"

"Let's just say that she's very busy and the taxes got overlooked," Sarah replied. "But it's taken care of now. The land is in my name, so I can handle any problems that come up. Thank you for your help, Mr. Nash."

"Call me Mace." He shook her hand. "I wish someone wanted to tackle setting all this up again. You know, there are still pumpkins growing in the field every fall. They're hard to get to, but they're the biggest ones you ever saw. The kids still sneak in here."

"No. I didn't know." She thought about the man she'd met in the field—Jack. "What about people squatting here? I met someone who said he lives here."

"Yeah. Sorry about that. I think he's an old friend of your grandfather's. Harmless, I'm sure. They were in the military together or some such. Sometimes he scares the kids while they're looking for pumpkins. They say he's not right in the head from his time in the war."

"Could you do something about that? And get the land cleared? I think between the weeds and the crazy man, most buyers would be scared off."

"Yes, ma'am. I can take care of that, and I'll have the power turned on by tomorrow so I can show the place at night if I need to. Good meeting you. I have your email and phone number. I'll let you know when the offers come in."

They shook hands. Sarah got in her rental car with Hunter and drove away.

She had to fight with herself not to look back. There was still one more sign for the pumpkin patch at the end of the road where it met the main highway. It had been the last sign she'd helped her grandmother draw and paint. The childish images of pumpkins and horses were done by her hand. They brought a smile to her face.

Her mother called as they headed toward the hotel in Suffolk. There were still no commercial lodgings in Misty River—only a gas station/convenience store, Nash Realty, and a sandwich shop. It had never grown more than that.

"Have you signed the papers?" her mother asked, obviously talking to someone else while she was on the phone. "When are you coming back?"

"The papers are signed," Sarah said. "I won't be back until sometime tomorrow. Hunter and I are seeing the sights and having dinner tonight before she has to head back to Charlotte."

"All right, sweetie. I'll see you when you get back. Your father got us tickets for that new exhibit at the art museum next week. Maybe we can have dinner at that French place you like so well."

Sarah rolled her eyes at Hunter as she turned on the

interstate. "You don't have to try to fill every minute of my day, right? I'm fine, Mom. I can handle being alone."

"I know you can. I saw that no-good ex-husband of yours today at the courthouse. You're lucky to be rid of him. There's someone better out there for you."

"Thanks. I'll talk to you later. Tell Dad I love him."

She knew both her parents were trying to smooth the transition from married to single for her. Her divorce had only been finalized a few weeks ago. But she and Alan hadn't lived together in more than two years. She loved them for worrying about her, but sometimes Alan already seemed like a distant memory of her past.

Hunter laughed. "You should've told her we were going to singles bars and hooking up with strippers."

"Yeah if I wanted her down here with me tonight! You know how she is."

"No worse than my mother. She's still trying to cope with Sam being gay. I think part of her still thinks he's going to become a surgeon like she always wanted, get married to the right girl, and have lots of babies."

Sarah knew she was right. She'd met Hunter and Sam at college. She'd had a huge crush on Sam. He was a couple of years younger than them, but he was gorgeous.

"How are you handling the break up? We haven't talked about it at all," Hunter pointed out.

"I know. What's left to say? We've gone over it a hundred times."

Sarah's marriage had been a tale of neither of them looking around enough before they got married. They'd gone to college together, attended the same parties. Their parents knew each other, and it was the most natural thing in the world to say 'yes' when Alan had proposed.

They'd had a huge wedding and a honeymoon in the Caribbean. They both had great jobs with big name law firms and a beautiful house. It seemed as though their future was assured.

Something had happened between the late hours they

worked and different ideas about what was important. Sarah had met Senator Clare Rosemond at a fundraiser and was immediately impressed by her. When the senator had offered her a job, she'd taken it without questioning what effect it would have on Alan. It had turned into a month-long argument that represented their differing viewpoints about the world. It seemed nothing was the same after.

Months before their married life was officially over, Alan was dating again. Sarah only wished him well, glad it was finally done.

She pulled the rental car into the parking spot she'd left before heading out to Misty River. The hotel was small and quiet, located on the Nansemond River. Hunter went to her room and Sarah checked her messages. There was nothing important.

A friend of Hunter's was on her way back to Charlotte, North Carolina from the Outer Banks. She was making a side trip to have dinner with them before she went home.

Sarah sighed as she saw the grass and wild flowers stuck in her hair. Her clothes were full of tick seeds and pulled by the thorns she'd walked through. Her face was sunburned, and her shoes were ruined from the muddy field.

It wasn't surprising that the crazy squatter hadn't taken her seriously.

She got in the shower to wash away the memories of that frightening encounter, but she couldn't get rid of her thoughts regarding the man. He said he knew that no one had lived there for sixteen years.

Was that the same teenage boy she remembered? He'd had a troubled home life, according to her grandparents. They'd asked him to stay with them when he couldn't go home. He'd helped out on the farm. She'd been jealous of him because she'd wanted to stay there too.

She couldn't remember his name. Could he still be living there? Had anyone questioned him about what happened to her grandparents? Had he been cleared of any possible wrongdoing in that regard?

It had been such a long time ago. Sarah lay back on her bed and closed her eyes.

She'd only been a child that August day when she couldn't find her grandparents. Her father had come to take her home while her mother had handled the police and whatever else had been done. No one ever talked about it much.

Between then and now had been filled with becoming an adult, school, and trying to figure out her own life. No questions that had formed in her younger mind had ever been answered. She'd mostly forgotten how terrible that day had been—until she'd stepped foot in Misty River again.

Suddenly she wanted all the answers and wasn't sure if she could go home to her normal life without knowing what had really happened to those people she'd loved so much. After all this time, was it possible to learn the truth?

Chapter Two

There was plenty of time before dinner to phone the county sheriff's office that represented Misty River and the surrounding areas. Sarah had no idea what had been done to find her grandparents or if the sheriff still considered their disappearance as an open case.

The deputy who answered the phone put her through to Sheriff Bill Morgan. They went through some small talk as he asked after her family and said he was happy to speak with her.

"That case has been in my file for so long that I've almost given up on it," he admitted. "There was never any evidence that Tommy and Bess didn't just decide to leave that night and never come back. I apologize if that idea is painful for you."

"Except, as I remember, their truck and car were still in the driveway."

"That's right, Ms. Tucker. It got to all of us that we couldn't find anything, no clue where they'd gone. There was some talk of aliens abducting them. That's how weird it was. George Burris is a writer from the local newspaper. He said something to that effect. I think he's retired now, but he might have a few answers."

Was he really referring her to a newspaper writer for answers?

"I was at the farm today and met a man who claimed to have been there since they disappeared. He said his name was Jack. Did you question him?"

"Jack. Sure, I know him. He wasn't a person of interest, if that's what you mean. He was just a boy at the time. We had no reason to suspect him."

In other words, no.

"I'd like to see the file you have on the investigation," she told him in clipped tones. "Can you have that ready for me tomorrow?"

"I can, Ms. Tucker, but I have to charge you thirty-five dollars for the copies. I'm sorry as I can be. The county needs to be reimbursed for their paper and such."

"That's fine. I'll be down at ten to pick it up." She thanked him and hung up. Her hands were shaking.

Sheriff Morgan wasn't much help. She'd known the case was old and probably hadn't even been looked at in years. But maybe fresh eyes would help. Maybe she could make a difference and finally know what happened to the two people who'd been so important in her life.

Sarah stared out of the hotel window. Suffolk was a nice city. She had good memories of growing up here. Her parents had moved to Richmond within six months of her grandparents' disappearance. It was as though the whole world had changed at that point, at least for her. Nothing had ever been the same.

She and her family had never gone back to Misty River. Sarah had assumed her mother had been in contact with the sheriff, but there were never updates that she'd shared.

With a plan in mind to change that veil of silence about that day, Sarah got ready for dinner and met Hunter at the car. She explained as much as she could to her friend. It wasn't an easy conversation.

They were having dinner at Al Forno Pizzeria. Sarah had already eaten there once and had recommended it for that night. Hunter introduced her friends when they arrived.

Dr. Peggy Lee, a forensic botanist, had bright red hair shot through with white. She was average height and weight and had inquisitive green eyes. Hunter told Sarah that Sam had given up on going to medical school to work with Peggy in her garden shop.

"Don't let her fool you," Peggy said with a smile. "Sam is only at *The Potting Shed* when he has to be. He'd spend all his time outside on the landscaping side of the business if he could."

Peggy introduced her husband, Steve Newsome, who worked for the FBI. He was a bit on the ordinary side—brown hair and eyes. Not someone you'd notice in a crowd. Sarah thought this might be part of his job working for the federal agency—being invisible in the shadows.

"I'm so glad you called, Hunter," Peggy said when they were seated at a table. "You wouldn't believe the crazy things that happened to us in Duck while we were there on vacation. Everyone went mermaid crazy. They even thought a man was murdered by mermaids!"

"Sounds crazy," Hunter said. "Did you see a mermaid?"

"No," Steve explained. "But other people did. When we left, there were people who'd just come to search for mermaids."

They all laughed as they enjoyed some wine.

"Maybe Steve can help you find out what happened to your grandparents," Hunter suggested. "Peggy and Steve are good at solving mysteries."

"I'm sure Steve doesn't want to talk shop while he's on vacation," Sarah uncomfortably demurred.

"Don't worry about it. I could use some shop talk after talking about sea turtles and mermaids all week." Steve smiled at her. "Tell me about your grandparents."

"It's a real thriller." Hunter nudged an elbow into Sarah's side. "She should option the movie rights to it."

The words came slowly at first then they poured out with all the emotion she'd felt at the time. When she was finished, she felt drained, but it was good to have said it out loud.

"You were very young at the time," Steve said when she'd finished. "Why this sudden interest?"

"I don't know. I can't explain why it hit me so hard today. I was just supposed to come down and sign some papers to sell the place. But I never got to ask questions about it. I'd like to know. Maybe it's time."

"I can understand that," he agreed. "I can't do anything formally, but I'll be happy to take a look at your information, if you like."

They planned a time to meet at the farm the next day so Steve could take a look around.

Sarah told them stories of spending time with her grandparents at the pumpkin patch. Once she'd started letting her memories out, it was like she couldn't stop. "I was there when a dozen baby goats were born one spring," she said. "Later that year, every time I talked to my grandmother, those goats were into everything. They ate all the beans and rampaged through the corn. One even got his head stuck inside a pumpkin."

They laughed and enjoyed their dinner. Steve wasn't as open and charming as Peggy, but Sarah was glad she'd met him anyway. She might never had said everything if he hadn't encouraged her.

Had her family stayed away from the subject because they all felt guilty for not finding out what happened? Sarah believed that was part of it for her and her mother. Maybe it was that feeling of paralysis that came with the sheriff and others telling them there was nothing they could do. If officials whose job it was to deal with these things couldn't help, what chance did they have?

Dinner lasted much longer than Sarah had anticipated. She and Hunter weren't back to the hotel until almost ten-thirty. Hunter was planning to leave by seven the next morning. But they sat and talked until one a.m. anyway. It was great catching up with her old friend. Hunter had recently broken up with a Charlotte police officer so they could commiserate with each other's love lives too.

The phone in her hotel room ringing woke her the next morning. She glanced at her cell phone, the normal means that her family or friends would have tried to get in touch with her. There were no messages or missed calls.

"Hello?" She cradled the hotel phone as she tried to pry her eyes open. It was only five a.m.

"Is this Sarah Tucker?" a husky, male voice asked.

"Yes. Who's this?"

"My name is George Burris. I used to work for the newspaper that served Misty River."

"How did you know where to find me, Mr. Burris?"

"I still have my sources in the community. I'd like to meet with you. I have ten years of information that I've gathered about your grandparents' disappearance. I think you should have it."

"All right. Where can I meet you?"

"It's not safe for me to meet you out in the open. Can you come to the pumpkin patch now?"

Not safe? "It's kind of late . . . early."

Sarah had an uneasy feeling about the call. The sheriff had mentioned Burris to her, but he was still a stranger. Yet if he really had more information about her grandparents, how could she say no? She felt like this was it—either she'd find out what had happened to them or she'd go home always wondering.

"It's important. I know you had the sheriff make copies of his file about them. That's how I knew you were in town and looking for answers. Believe me, my information is a hundred times more in depth than anything he has."

She glanced at her watch again, torn between wanting to meet with him and feeling vulnerable doing it alone. She didn't want to wake Hunter since she had a long drive ahead of her. "What about later in the morning?"

"It's now or never." He seemed to repeat her thoughts back at her. "You don't realize how much I'm putting my life on the line to help you. Do you want the answers or not?"

"Okay. I want the answers."

"I'll meet you there in thirty minutes. If you're not there, the answers leave with me."

He hung up abruptly. Sarah looked at the phone, trying to figure out if what he was talking about was worth the risk. Maybe he was as crazy as the squatter. Sheriff Morgan had said Burris had suggested alien abduction.

But she had to take the chance.

"And this time I won't be fooled into letting go of my gun," she promised herself as she reloaded the bullets. She wasn't completely sure she could shoot someone, but she could at least scare him and run away.

After changing clothes into jeans, boots, and a T-shirt, she left her room.

It was dark and quiet outside. She could see the lights on a boat as it cruised down the river. *This is crazy. I should turn around and go back inside.*

But she knew she was going.

She wanted someone to know where she'd gone. She left a message at the front desk for Hunter in case she came to say goodbye. Her parents would know where to look for her, too, if something happened.

Once she was behind the wheel and on her way back out to Misty River, she continued to berate herself for agreeing to meet this man before dawn at what was left of the farm. The property was a mile off the main road that ran through the middle of town. If the squatter was there, and dangerous, despite Sheriff Morgan's opinion of him, she was out of luck.

"And definitely out of your element," she told herself in the rearview mirror as her heart pumped nervously. "You're not even a criminal attorney. You know this is stupid. But here you are."

Knowing it could be dangerous didn't stop her from

turning the rental car off the main road toward the farm. The sign for the pumpkin patch that she and her grandmother had drawn had been amusing and nostalgic during the day. In the dim five-thirty morning light, it just looked creepy.

She hoped George Burris might be in a car waiting in the driveway for her with his headlights on. They'd meet, and he'd hand her a package through the window without her ever leaving the relative safety of her car. It would be like a TV movie with a happy ending—there was a terrible mix-up but her grandparents were alive and well.

There was a car in the driveway. It was backed in, but there were no headlights and no one inside as she drove up to it.

"Now what?" She was parked but still gripping the steering wheel.

She rolled open a window and called his name, but there was no reply. She wanted to hit herself in the head for not getting his cell phone number. She didn't want to walk through a hundred and eighty acres in the middle of the night looking for him.

That's when she noticed a moving light inside the house. Maybe it was a candle or a flashlight. He had to be in there. Holding her gun in a savage grip, she locked the car and crept warily up to the house.

There was no moon in the clear sky above her. There had been outdoor lights in various spots around the farm when her grandparents had lived here. Now everything was dark. She wished she had a flashlight, but she'd left her cell phone in the car. She started to go back and get it but was afraid she'd lose her nerve and leave.

She followed the old, cracked sidewalk that led to the front door. She hoped the light in the house was George Burris and not Jack the crazy squatter.

It doesn't matter. She was ready to confront either of them. She was having a hard time breathing, but she tried to stay focused on the house and the light.

Sarah was near the gazebo where her grandparents had

always displayed whatever seasonal produce was available for sale. Her grandmother had liked to dress it up for each time of year—holly and a fir tree for Christmas, pumpkins and skeletons for Halloween. She knew the stairs to the front porch were nearby. She could almost see them in the dim starlight.

Then something large and dark jumped in front of her. She stopped breathing for a moment and almost forgot to bring the gun up in front of her.

"Back so soon?" Jack's voice was soft. "I see you're armed again. You're stubborn, aren't you?"

"Stay back." She tried to keep her voice authoritative. "I don't want to hurt you."

"I'm not worried about it." He tapped the gun with a careless finger. "Is that thing even loaded this time?"

"Yes. Get out of my way."

"I guess you know who's in the house, huh?"

"I do. Now get out of here. I warned you already. I put the property up for sale. Things are going to be different now. I don't think the realtor wants you showing up while he's trying to sell it."

"I think I was clear that I'm not leaving."

She couldn't see his face, but he was obviously certain about his part in all this. Maybe it was time to shake him up. What would it take to get rid of him?

"Sheriff Morgan is interested in talking to you about what happened to my grandparents. You might not want to stick around for a new investigation into their disappearance."

"It's about time." His words were snarky. "Did seeing the old place make you feel guilty, Sarah?"

"I don't feel guilty. And I don't have to explain anything to you. But since you were nice enough to tell me that you were here when my grandparents vanished, I can tell you that the sheriff thinks you might be a suspect that was overlooked in the initial investigation."

It wasn't true, but it was something she hoped would

scare him off. The man really was crazy to stand there arguing with her as she held a loaded gun on him. She longed to ask him if he was the same teenager she remembered from when she was twelve but couldn't find a way to say it.

He laughed in a slow, non-humorous way. It sounded more like a threat. "Are you scared, Sarah? You should be."

She was about to go into legal mode, offering arguments about why it was illegal for him to be there, when a loud crack split the morning around them. It was followed rapidly by another loud crack—gunfire—and the sound of shattering glass.

Sarah knew that sound. She'd lived around guns all her life. She'd barely processed the information that someone might be shooting at her when Jack knocked her down to the soft grass and put himself on top of her like a human shield.

"Someone's shooting." She was almost as surprised that he would try to protect her as she was about the gunfire.

"Stay down. I don't think that was meant for you, but let's not take any chances."

"Hey!" she complained when he took her gun again. "What am I supposed to use to protect myself?"

"Don't move. You won't have to do anything. Let me take a look around."

"I think the bullet hit the front window."

But Jack was gone. She argued with herself about listening to him and staying down or going to the house to see what was going on. Why was he so annoyingly arrogant? And why wasn't he afraid the sheriff might think he was responsible for her grandparents' disappearance?

The area was quiet again except for the hoot of an owl and a few crickets. Sarah waited impatiently in the dew-damp grass for a minute then got to her knees to look around.

She couldn't see Jack or any other large shadow that might indicate another human ready to take a shot. The dim light was still in the window. It was probably an off-season hunter whose bullet had travelled farther than he'd expected in the open fields surrounding the house. It wouldn't be the first time.

Having argued herself into feeling safe, and embarrassed that Jack had pushed her down, Sarah got to her feet and brushed the grass from her jeans and shirt. She kept her head low as she surveyed the yard again. There was only her car and the empty one that had been there when she'd arrived. It seemed safe to her.

"I told you to stay down." Jack was immediately at her side. "I think whoever fired that shot took off, but there's no way to know for sure if anyone else is out here besides us."

"Is that George in the house? How did he get inside?"

"Why don't we go in and ask him? It will be safer for you in there anyway."

"It was probably just an overzealous hunter," she told him as he hurried her toward the front door. "Did you find the broken window?"

"I'm afraid so." He opened the front door. A heavyset man lay on the front room rug. "I guess someone didn't want you to talk to George."

Chapter Three

"Someone shot him on purpose?" She gulped as she saw the blood on the thin green carpet in the dim lantern light.

"I'd say so." He nodded toward the hole in the broken window. "Why was he here, Sarah?"

"He called me at the hotel. He said he knew things about my grandparents that he hadn't shared with the sheriff. He offered to give me the information." She didn't even think not to answer him. There was a dead man on the floor in front of her.

"This must be what he wanted you to have." Jack scooped a manila folder off the floor and handed it to her. "You're in luck. Whoever shot George wasn't worried about you."

Sarah's head was spinning. She tried to swallow hard but couldn't and threw up on the floor next to George Burris. "I'm sorry. This is more than I bargained for."

Jack led her into the kitchen, using the lantern to find their way. "I suppose so. I can get some water from the hand pump outside. The water in here has been turned off for years. Stay here."

She wanted to argue with him but literally didn't have the stomach for it. She stayed where she was in the empty kitchen, staring at the wood floor, until he returned.

"Where's your phone?" He handed her a wet rag. "You should call this in."

"In…in the car."

She wiped the cool rag across her face. Jack had moved the battery-powered lantern to the kitchen table. The glow from it spread around the room. The last time she'd seen this room it had looked as though her grandparents had just stepped away. She still expected it to be the same as when she was twelve—cornbread on the stove and coffee perking.

"Are you okay?" He crouched beside her and looked up into her face. "At least you don't look like you're going to faint. You were kind of pale back there. I haven't caught an unconscious woman in my arms for a while. Not sure I know how anymore."

"I never faint." But her head was still spinning, and her stomach threatened to rebel again.

"There's that angry woman with the gun that I met yesterday."

She smiled despite herself. "Speaking of which, do you still have my gun? It's annoying the way you're always taking it from me."

He handed it back to her. "If you stay around long enough, I'll teach you a trick so no one disarms you again."

That brought Sarah to her senses. What had she gotten herself into?

She hadn't stopped to consider the wisdom of letting sleeping dogs lie, as her grandfather used to say. Now not only were her grandparents gone, there was a dead man in their living room. She was going to have to call the sheriff and probably be here for an extra day or two at least. What had she been thinking?

"I'm not staying any longer than I have to," she told him.

"Thanks for the offer, but I have a home and a life to get back to. Why would anyone want to kill Mr. Burris because he had sixteen-year-old information about my grandparents? Sheriff Morgan made him sound like a crackpot."

"Maybe we should take a look at what George brought with him," Jack suggested. "Are you up to that now?"

"I guess I better be." She took a deep breath. "But you're right. I should call the sheriff first."

"It will take him at least forty minutes to get out here," he advised as he opened the folder on the table. "Plenty of time to look inside."

Sarah was torn between leaving him with the folder and going to get her phone. She felt like snatching it from him so he wouldn't see what George had brought for her. It could be information that implicated Jack in her grandparents' disappearance. For all she knew, Jack had shot George before she even got there and pretended that they were in danger. The whole thing could be a set up. She certainly didn't know him well enough to trust him.

She moaned and put her head in her hands. "I'm afraid I'm going to be sick again. Could you get the cell phone? It's in the front seat." She tossed him the keys. "Thanks."

"Sure."

As he was going out the door, Sarah opened the folder. She barely glanced inside before she felt her stomach roiling again. There had been a few newspaper clippings and pictures in it. Not much. Maybe when she had more time to study it.

"That's okay if you take a look without me," he drawled, setting her cell phone on the table. "I looked at all your phone information before I brought it in. We're even. But that was kind of sneaky. I like it."

She called 911 and looked up to see his bearded face close to hers. "Why are you here really? Are you mentally damaged like Mace Nash said? Do you need money to move on?"

He sat at the table with her. "I might be deranged, but I

don't need your money. I'm here because I made a promise to your grandfather that I intend to keep. Until then, this is my home."

That drove her even crazier. "What kind of promise? Are you the same kid who was here right before they disappeared?"

He slid the file away from her and began sorting through the contents. "Better hope the sheriff gets here fast. He might not believe your story if George is already cold."

"What about you?" she demanded. "What's your story going to be?"

"I don't expect to be here. He and I have talked before. I don't see any reason to do it again."

"They'll think I'm responsible for this."

"With that little toy?" He grinned at the gun on the table. "Hardly. It sounded like a Ruger to me—maybe a 77. It makes a loud report like the one we heard."

"The sheriff might think you killed George." She wanted to see the smug look disappear from his face, but she was disappointed.

"Not if he's smart." He put the file back on the table. "Why would someone want to kill George? What did he know that the killer didn't want him sharing with you?"

"I don't know. Since you claim to know my grandparents, you know they were simple farmers who made a living from this place like a lot of other farmers. I know it seems mysterious that they just left, but I don't think there are any deep, dark secrets about it."

His blue eyes stayed on hers. "So you think George is dead because there was no secret to hide. Good observation."

Sarah bristled at his sarcastic tone. "Okay. If you're so much smarter, why would anyone kill George over what's in this almost twenty-year-old file?"

"Because someone has something important to hide that he thought George was about to expose. He didn't kill you because he doesn't expect you to understand what it is. He's not even worried about the sheriff seeing what's in here. But there's something we're missing. People don't go out in the middle of the night and shoot people for no reason—at least not around here."

She didn't know how to counter that and still worried about her involvement in the shooting. "I'll give everything to the sheriff. He can take it from there."

"Good plan. Do that. Leave town. You're bound to be safe. You won't find out what happened to Tommy and Bess. But you'll be safe."

"You know something more than you're saying too." She thought about his accusations and the promise he'd made to her grandfather. "No one makes a promise to someone and lives off the land after that promise should have been invalid. Come on. They've been gone sixteen years. When does your promise end?"

His hard chin went up. "When I say it does."

They both heard the sound of approaching sirens. It would only be a few minutes now.

Sarah put her gun and phone on the table. "It must be time for you to run away. Otherwise you might not like what the sheriff has to say. And a friend of mine from the FBI is coming to take a look at the investigation so far. He might want to talk to you too."

"Are you trying to get rid of me already? And after I saved your life. You could at least pretend to be grateful."

There was a stiff knock on the front door followed by a bellowing voice from outside. The sirens were still coming toward them. It wasn't Sheriff Morgan yet.

Sarah went to see who was there, thinking the killer would be unlikely to knock on the door and demand admittance. She knew she was right when she confronted a man in his worn overalls and a T-shirt standing in front of her.

"Can I help you?" she asked him.

"I hope so. It's not hunting season. Are you the new owner of this place? I live over yonder. We don't like loud noises this time of morning. Throws the cows off. How about you keep it down?"

She glanced at the driveway. There were still only two cars. The older man had walked through the field to reach the house. He was serious about his peace and quiet.

"I'm sorry. Someone was shooting. It wasn't me. The sheriff is on his way."

The man sat on the top step. "Good. I want to register a complaint. All that shooting scared my horses. A couple of them ran off. It'll take me most of today to get them back. You people from the city think you can come out here and party down at all hours of the day and night. We'll see about that."

Sarah hid a smile as she turned to see if Jack found the conversation humorous too. But he was gone. The kitchen was empty—he'd taken George Burris's file with him. What was she going to tell Sheriff Morgan now? At least the file made sense of her early morning meeting.

She closed the front door and sat on the top step with the man in his overalls. "Did you know Tommy and Bess?"

"Of course. I've lived here all of my life. Good people. The aliens got them. I keep hoping they bring them back."

"Aliens?"

"Sure. How else did they disappear that way—unless you believe in government conspiracies?" He squinted at her. "Lots of people in Misty River think the government took them. Who knows where? I hope they're happy out there if that's what happened."

"When was the last time you saw them?" Sarah was making this up as she went along. But who better to know than this nosey neighbor? She didn't remember him, but she ignored most adults when she was twelve.

"Let me think." He scratched his head. "I believe I saw Tommy outside talking to Jack the day before they disappeared."

"Jack?" She picked up quickly. "You know Jack?"

"Sure. He's a big help during foaling. Nobody calmer with the mares than him."

The deputies' cars were noisy coming down the road. Sarah took a deep breath and got to her feet. Jack was a busy man—popping up when she got here, helping his neighbor with foals, and stealing her information before ducking out. She wanted to see the sheriff's reaction to what she had to say about him.

"Thanks for your help," she said to her neighbor. "I'm Sarah Tucker, Bess and Tommy's granddaughter."

He slowly got to his feet. "I'm Grayson Pope. I'm glad someone from the family finally came back to take care of this place. You know, when Tommy and I were young, there was only our farms for miles around. I took over from my father and my grandfather. Tommy did the same. Too bad there was no man born in your family. Women make bad farmers."

Sarah watched him shuffle off to complain to a large man getting out of his car. Would it help her case if she could use Grayson Pope as a witness?

"Ms. Tucker, I assume." The large man in uniform shook hands with her neighbor and then removed his cowboy hat when he reached her. "Sheriff Bill Morgan, ma'am. What's going on out here?"

They walked through the house together, the sheriff holding the flashlight, as he took a quick look at George Burris' body on the living room floor. He asked her if there was any coffee when they reached the kitchen.

"I don't live here, sheriff," Sarah said. "I only came down to pay the back taxes and put the property up for sale."

"Too bad." He yawned. "I could use a cup." He glanced around the kitchen. "Where's Jack? I thought for sure he'd be here."

"The man is a squatter on my grandparents' farm," she reminded him in a sharp tone. "Shouldn't it be your job to remove him?"

He took offense, his eyes narrowing in his tan face. "Don't come down here and presume to tell me what my job is, Ms. Tucker. No one from the family gave a crap all these years about this place falling apart. At least Jack cuts the grass sometimes. He did more to honor Tommy and Bess's memory than their family."

She was amazed by his reply and his casual acceptance of the man breaking the law on her property. For a moment she was speechless.

"So what's the story here?" Sheriff Morgan took the opportunity to question her. "Why is George dead in your house?"

This was happening so fast that she felt the need to sit again. At least she'd stopped vomiting. That had been embarrassing. She'd thought she was made of sterner stuff.

Sarah explained how the newspaper reporter had called her and asked to meet at the house. "He said he had better information about my grandparents than you did—which was also what you told me."

"He was probably right. George always seemed to be part rat. He could find tiny bits of information that he used to make the rest of us look bad. What happened then? You didn't like something he had to say so you shot him?"

"What?" She put a hand to her forehead. Wasn't this exactly what she'd been afraid of that Jack had laughed off? "Of course I didn't shoot him. I was standing outside and someone shot him through the front window. You saw the body." She showed him her tiny gun. "I couldn't have done it with this."

"I was just joking with you. It took something big to do that damage. Probably someone didn't want George spilling the beans, bless his soul." He took the gun from her anyway. "What happened to the information he promised you?"

"It was here, but Jack walked out with it."

He grinned. "I knew old Jack was here. Did he know who the killer was?"

"If he did, he didn't say. But he took the folder that we found on the floor with Mr. Burris. I barely had a chance to look at it. Maybe that warrants you searching the property until you get the folder. That might have some clues as to who killed him."

"It might at that," Sheriff Morgan replied. "But Jack will see we get it back. Why did you agree to meet George out here? A sudden interest in what happened to your grandparents? Guilty conscience?"

"I guess you could call it that. I was just a kid when they disappeared. When I got back, I started wondering what happened all over again. If that's a crime, then I'm guilty."

He pressed the button on the radio he wore on his shoulder. "Go on and come in," he instructed his people. "Give the crime scene folks a call."

Sarah waited in the kitchen as the living room was flooded with deputies and flashlights. She felt completely out of her depth. She knew nothing about homicide proceedings besides what she'd read in books or seen in movies.

The sheriff had looked at her phone and taken her driver's license with her gun. He'd told her to wait, treating her more like a criminal than an innocent bystander. He didn't seem interested in talking to Jack at all. Sheriff Morgan was clearly on Jack's side. It was crazy to her that everyone knew Jack was here but no one did anything to remedy the situation.

A good-looking deputy with the name *Broadwell* on his nametag brought her phone and license back with apologies that the sheriff was keeping the gun for testing. "Is there anything else I can do for you, ma'am? We're here to serve."

Sarah thanked him. His flirting brought a smile to her lips, despite the trying night she'd had. "No, thanks. I'm fine."

He tipped his hat and left her. Sarah dialed her mother's phone number with a shaky hand. She probably should have called her to keep from making this mistake in the first place. Thinking back on it, she should have stayed at the hotel. Her mother would have told her as much.

"It looks like I'm going to be at least another day or two," she began her explanation when her mother's sleepy voice answered.

"Sarah, it's barely six a.m.," her mother said. "What's going on out there?"

"I'm not sure, Mom, but I might be a suspect in a murder."

Chapter Four

Sarah fell asleep at the table waiting for the sheriff and his deputies to finish their work in the house. When she awakened, there was the smell of coffee in the air and a pillow under her head. Because George Burris's file had been returned, she knew Jack had done those things. The man needed a bell around his neck.

She located a dish towel in the pantry and went outside. The sun was finally up and the sky was clear. Everything seemed better.

It took a little doing, but she finally found the hand pump by following a path where the tall grass had been flattened. The water was cool and fresh. She wiped her face and washed her hands, feeling much more herself afterward.

Inside, she rummaged in the cabinet until she found one of her grandmother's old coffee cups. It had strawberries on it, as did her plates. Her grandmother had loved strawberries. Sarah poured herself a cup of coffee from the old percolator-type pot on the stove. She wasn't sure if she'd ever had better.

The power was on now—lights were on in the kitchen and the living room. Mace was as good as his word.

As she drank the coffee, and wished for a donut, Sheriff Morgan returned to the kitchen.

"Ms. Tucker, we're finished for now. Try not to go into that room. You never know when the crime scene people might want to take another look."

"That's fine. I'm meeting someone here shortly, but then I'm headed back to the hotel in Suffolk."

He glanced around the kitchen. "I shared many a cup of coffee here with Bess and Tommy."

She held up the pot. "Would you like some?"

"Sure. Thanks." He took a seat as she dusted off another cup.

"I don't have cream or sugar," she warned.

"Not a problem."

Sarah put the cup in front of him, and he thanked her before taking a sip.

"There's some chicory in that, huh?"

"Maybe. I'm not sure what chicory is. The coffee was here when I woke up."

He chuckled. "Good old Jack."

"Tell me something, Sheriff Morgan. What is it about this man squatting on my property that everyone loves so much?"

"Jack's one of the good ones," he said. "I'd trust him with my daughter, which is saying a lot for me."

"I get that. And he's good with foaling mares, according to Mr. Pope next door. But he keeps popping up, scaring the crap out of me. He acts like he owns the farm. I had planned to call you and have him arrested if he wouldn't leave on his own."

He lost a lot of his mellow mood at her words. "You want me to arrest Jack for doing what your grandparents asked him to do? That hardly seems fair."

Maybe now they were getting to the heart of it. "What

did they ask him to do?"

"Keep an eye on the farm, of course. He won't let anyone hunt here, and chases off trespassers. Do you think this house would look as good as it does after all these years if Jack hadn't been here? Windows get broken by birds, and teenagers look for spots like this to hang out. Some people think this place is haunted because of Jack. Nobody comes here."

"How do you know they asked him to watch the place? How do you know he didn't kill them and bury them somewhere under all that grass?"

"I take his word for it since he's been here all these years. No offense, but your mother sure wasn't interested in the farm. She made that clear from the time she was a young'un. Then there was you and your brother. The two of you never came back after the day Tommy and Bess disappeared. Jack and I both figured you'd sell the place off. And here you are."

Sarah took a sip of her coffee. "We were very young when it happened. My brother, Dusty, was only seven. I'm not sure he even remembers this place."

"That's what I mean."

"So Jack's plan is to take care of the farm until my grandparents come back?"

"Something like that." He shrugged. "He's a man of his word. He's taken care of the old pumpkin patch. You know there are still pumpkins growing out there. I guess they reseed themselves every year. Jack lets a few people come out here and pick some. No reason all of them should go bad. Tommy loved that patch."

Sarah felt as though she understood a little more about why Jack was there. But it wasn't like he was a member of the family. She was grateful to him for keeping up with the house and not letting people come in and tear it apart. Maybe once it was sold, he'd find another place to live.

"I gotta get going." Sheriff Morgan got to his feet. "I'm beat. I need a shower and some fresh clothes before I start the day. My wife is keeping breakfast warm—biscuits and eggs. You're welcome to come home with me and eat. She always makes extra."

"I have to change too, but thanks." She held out the file that Jack had returned. "I haven't really looked at it, but you can have it if you think it will help you catch Mr. Burris's killer."

"Thanks. I have the file I promised you in the car."

"Thank you. I'll walk you out."

They went through the back door and around the house. A red rose vine was growing up the side of the porch. The roses were beautiful, deep and red. Their perfume was heavy in the early morning air. Sarah remembered it because she had frequently snagged her clothes on it when she was a kid. She had always run around the corner without looking.

The sun was coming up across the tall grass that surrounded the house. It made everything take on a golden hue with the sky bright blue above it. A light breeze rippled through the trees near the river and shivered in the grass.

Sheriff Morgan gave her the folder he'd brought. "This is all the information we have on your grandparents' disappearance. I don't know what you're looking for, but I hope it's in there."

"Thank you. I don't know what I'm looking for either," she admitted. "I'm not sure I'd know if I saw it. I just wish I could walk away from this place with some closure."

"I understand. But don't plan on going anywhere besides your hotel for the next few days, huh? We need to settle on what happened to George. You're a witness, even if you don't realize it."

"I hate to sound like I'm saying the same thing over and over, but Jack was here too. Doesn't that make him a witness as well?"

He nodded. "I'll talk to him. And I'll see you around, Ms. Tucker. Would you mind writing down your cell phone number and the name of the hotel where you're staying? Just put it on this paper here."

Sarah put her information on the pad of paper that said *Sheriff's Department* and then watched him leave. Did he really think she had something to do with Mr. Burris's death or was he just trying to keep her around? She hadn't known the dead man—but maybe the sheriff really believed she'd seen something that could help ID George Burris's killer.

There was a loud machinery noise coming down the road toward her. It was Mr. Pope on a large black tractor that was towing something behind it that looked like an instrument of torture.

"Morning," he yelled over the noise when he reached her. "Where do you want me to start?"

"I'm not sure what you mean," she yelled back. "Where do I want you to start what?"

"Jack said you might want to get some of this grass cut down." He laughed. "He said it would make you feel safer if you could see him sneaking up on you. That man's a card, isn't he?"

Sarah pursed her lips and started to refuse. Jack couldn't go around telling people what he thought she might want them to do. But it would be nice to have the grass cut, even if she was only staying a few extra days. She'd have to pay for it herself, of course, instead of Mace paying for it to help the land sell faster. He would have charged it back to her anyway when the house was sold.

"Yes. He has an amazing sense of humor. Thanks. I appreciate you offering to cut the grass. How much do I owe you?"

"You don't owe me nothin'. Jack said he's gonna help with my barn-raising this weekend. That covers it."

She started to disagree, but Mr. Pope had already pulled down his ball cap and started through the yard like a bulldog chasing a rabbit.

"Maybe he's right." She watched the tractor mow down the tall grass and weeds. "Maybe he won't be able to sneak around as much."

"What did Sheriff Morgan say?" Jack asked.

Sarah spun around. "Stop doing that." She focused on the man in front of her. "It looks like I'm going to have to be in town for a few more days. I don't know how much of that time I'll be here, but I'd appreciate it if you quit sneaking up on me."

"No more sneaking up." He nodded, following where her eyes had been on the tractor. "But you did look really cute drooling on the kitchen table this morning."

She self-consciously swiped at the corners of her mouth. "Yeah. Thanks for the coffee anyway."

"Did you have a chance to look at the file?"

"No. I gave it to the sheriff. You were wrong. He thinks *I* killed Mr. Burris."

"I don't think that's true. He probably just wants to keep an eye on you. Whoever killed George could come after you."

She hadn't thought of that idea. "Well I guess it's good I'm not staying at the house."

"I was surprised you were still here."

"I'm meeting someone or I wouldn't be. It would be nice if you could stay out of the way. My friend is with the FBI. He's going to help me look for my grandparents."

The last was wishful on her part. Steve had already made it clear that he wasn't using his FBI's resources. She didn't know how much help he was actually offering.

Jack's blue eyes went slowly from her feet to her head. "Looking like that? You better change clothes. He might think you killed George too."

She stared belligerently at his heavily bearded face—he was wearing the same clothes he'd been wearing yesterday. He had a lot of nerve making remarks about what she looked like when he was such a mess.

But she held her tongue. She didn't want to get into anything that personal with him. Let him say what he wanted. She didn't care.

"I'm going back to the hotel. Maybe you should make yourself scarce if you don't want to answer questions."

"Maybe I should. You know, I don't remember you being so mouthy when you were a kid."

"A kid?" She stared at him. "I *knew* it was you under that hair and beard. Did you see what happened to my grandparents, Jack? Were you here when they left?" Tears rose unbidden in her eyes.

"My dad came for me that night after you went home. Whatever happened was the following weekend right before you came back." He shrugged. "I was sent to live with relatives in West Virginia until I joined the military. I came back looking for Tommy and Bess two years later. No one knew where they were."

Sarah barely recognized the man in front of her as the gawky boy in blue jeans she had run wild with sometimes when she visited. Her eyes narrowed on his lean face. "How old were you?"

"Fourteen. They took me in when my father went on a binge. I stayed here until he came for me."

"I was twelve." She sighed. "Did they really ask you to keep an eye on the farm?"

"Yes." His eyes wandered back to her. "Want to take a look at the pumpkins before you get all dolled up for the FBI?"

She glanced at her watch. There was plenty of time. "I would. Sheriff Morgan said there were still pumpkins every year. He said you let people pick them."

"Better than watching them rot on the vine. Come on."

She followed him down a path that led between the tall grasses. It looked as though he used it frequently since there was nothing but dirt from the house to the barn. She recalled that he used to sleep in there on a blanket and straw.

And she suddenly remembered that he had kissed her in the barn—her first kiss. Her face got hot with the thought. How had she forgotten about it? Did he remember?

The path opened into the pumpkin patch her grandparents had nurtured for so many years. No grass or weeds grew here—just hundreds of orange pumpkins in all sizes and shapes. Some of them were huge—she could remember climbing in and out of a pumpkin shell when she was very young. The vines and leaves were thick and green, shading the plants during the hottest summer day.

"I guess you take care of this too, huh?" She let her gaze go from pumpkin to pumpkin, admiring each one.

"You could say that. They plant themselves every year. That's the heavy lifting. I just make sure they survive."

She stopped staring at the acres of pumpkins and looked at him. "Why?"

"Because there was no one else."

"I don't mean to be rude, but you seem of sound mind and body." Her eyes went up and down his tall, muscular frame. "Why would you do this for people who weren't even your family? What if they never come back?"

"They were like my family but better. Tommy asked me to keep an eye on the place. That's what I did when I came home from the Army and they were gone."

"I don't know if that was what he meant. I'm sure he didn't mean that you should make it your life. Wasn't there somewhere else you wanted to go? Someone you wanted to be with?"

"We'd better get going if you want to change before your FBI friend gets here."

"Wait, Jack. Can't you give me a straight answer? I know you don't plan to live here forever."

"Someone should."

"But that may not happen. It's a lot of work running a farm. I might not be able to sell the place. What will you do?"

The sound of Mr. Pope's tractor getting close to them diverted her attention. When she looked back, Jack was gone again. She swore softly under her breath and waited where she was so that Mr. Pope didn't accidentally mow her down too. He might not be able to see the top of her head through the grass.

He stopped as he saw the pumpkin patch and turned off

the noisy tractor. "It's hot for September." He put a flask to his mouth and chugged water. "I'm surprised you could even see this place from the house. Looks like a good pumpkin harvest this year. Tommy and Bess would've been pleased."

They sat for a while near the gate that marked where the pumpkins grew. Mr. Pope talked about growing organic lettuce and spinach.

"Organic. That's where the money is right now—except for the farm-to-fork stuff. There's good money in feeding people without having thousands of acres of corn. You have to think small and local. Big movement to locally grown foods, you know."

She didn't, not really. She'd stopped at a few produce stands back home when she had to leave the city for one reason or another. She hadn't really thought much about farmers growing food, despite her background.

"I'm not sure my grandparents really ever made any money on the pumpkin patch."

"Are you kidding me?" He took off his baseball cap and wiped his brow with a red rag he wore around his neck. "Kids came out here from all the schools in the area. They rode the hay wagons out to pick their pumpkins, and then they brought their parents back. They bought food to feed the sheep and goats, and then Bess sold them her jams and jellies. They did okay. Not a fortune, if that's what you're thinking, but it was a good living and a good life."

Sarah thanked him for his point of view. She liked thinking that her grandparents had done well here and would never have simply deserted the place. All of her childhood memories weren't wrong.

"Ms. Tucker?" Mace yelled from the house. "Are you out there? Looks like I have a buyer for the property."

Chapter Five

Sarah followed the path back to the house as she heard Mr. Pope restart the tractor.

Mace was waiting on the porch for her. A tow truck with a sheriff's escort was hooking up Mr. Burris's car, presumably to take it in for evidence.

"I heard what happened up here last night," he said. "Not to worry. Our buyer doesn't care. He called me right after I listed the property. Maybe five minutes later. I'm sure you'll find his offer better than you might've expected."

Sarah took a look at the offer he already had in writing from the buyer. "That's a lot more than I was asking."

"You're telling me." He grinned. "We could get this over right away. I could have the papers drawn up today. What do you think?"

It was a very good deal. Her brother and mother would share in the profits, and they would be pleased with what she'd done. She had the power to make the decision about the sale. There was nothing stopping her from taking the money and going home—well, when Sheriff Morgan said it was okay for her to go.

"Should I call my lawyer and find out if I can sell the property with an ongoing police investigation taking place?" she asked

"I don't see the problem if the buyer doesn't care." His words were emphasized by his toothy smile. "Come on. We can ask my lawyer while he draws up the sales documents."

Sarah looked out at the property that was beginning to take form as Mr. Pope's tractor cut the grass. It was starting to look more like she remembered. Not that her memories of the place had anything to do with her selling it. She'd known when she came here today that her emotions would be stirred up again seeing the farm. They were stronger than she thought they would be. But she was still there to sell it, and she probably wouldn't get a better deal.

"All right." She saw Peggy and Steve pull into the driveway. She'd missed her chance to change clothes. "Some friends of mine are here. Maybe we could meet after lunch."

Mace glanced at his large-numbered watch. "It's barely eight-thirty, Ms. Tucker. This is a good deal. Maybe you could talk to your friends after we finalize everything."

"They came out from Suffolk as a favor to me. If this is a motivated buyer, he won't mind waiting until after lunch." What was the hurry anyway? The property had been here a long time. Another day or even two shouldn't matter in the long run.

"Are you willing to take that chance?" He pushed harder to have her see his point of view. "When word of George Burris's death in the house gets around, a lot of other people won't be interested."

Sarah expected him to be aggressive since this sale would mean extra money in his pocket, but she wasn't going to be shoved into a deal she wasn't ready for. "Later. I'll call you when my friends leave."

He started to say something else, thought better of it, and pulled out his cell phone as he walked back to his car.

"You're busy out here today," Peggy said with a smile. "Having work done on the property?"

"Not exactly, except for having the grass mowed. I'm afraid something else happened early this morning." Sarah told them about the call she got from Mr. Burris and being shot at when she came to meet with him. "At least I think someone was shooting at me. I'm not sure. Whoever it was shot him right through the living room window."

Steve frowned. "Has local law enforcement been here?"

"A long time ago. They just took Mr. Burris's car. I don't know if I'm a serious suspect or not. The sheriff asked me not to leave town. Then the real estate agent told me he's already sold the property."

"It sounds like a TV movie," Peggy remarked. "Why would you be a suspect at all? You said you'd never met the man who died."

"But she called him for information and agreed to meet him here," Steve said. "I'd like a good look at her, too, if it was my case."

"I'd still like to talk to you about my grandparents," Sarah said. "I have some coffee in the kitchen, and the file that Sheriff Morgan gave me about the investigation. Will you take a look at it?"

"Sure," Steve said. "Walk me through what happened to your grandparents. Then I'll take a look at the file."

Sarah did what he asked as well as she could remember it. "My mother was dropping me off for a few days. Usually she didn't even go inside with me, but she'd just gotten a new job in Richmond and wanted to tell my grandmother about it. The back door was open. Their car and truck were in the yard, just like normal. I ran in the house and called them. Everything was just like they were about to sit down and eat, but we couldn't find them."

"And your mother called the sheriff?"

"Yes. We waited in the car until he got here. My mother made me stay out there for a long time while she talked to him. A few more police cars got here. They spent a lot of time in the house and then started searching outside. They even brought dogs. But as far as I know, no one has ever seen them again."

Peggy put her hand on Sarah's shoulder. "That had to be terrible for you. Were those your mother's parents?"

"Yes. Her maiden name was Denning. Her parents were Bess and Tommy Denning. She's an only child. I don't remember what it was like for her to find them gone. I was too busy feeling sorry for myself, I guess."

"You were a child," Peggy said. "I can't imagine you feeling any different."

"What happened after that?" Steve asked as they walked toward the house. "I'm guessing tons of law enforcement and finally private investigators."

Sarah opened the back door into the kitchen. "My mother never discussed it with me, but I remember hearing her and my father talking about it, arguing about it. There wasn't an answer to their questions, and eventually they stopped discussing it."

He glanced around the kitchen. "So everything looked completely normal when you came in that day? You didn't notice anything unusual. No odd smells or something out of place?"

She closed her eyes and thought back to that awful day. "Nothing was different. I'd walked in a hundred times the same way."

"Describe it," he urged.

"There were plates and food on the table. I touched the cornbread that was on the stove. It was still warm. The coffee pot was hot. I expected one of them to come downstairs or come in from outside at any minute. It just never happened." She wiped tears from her eyes.

Peggy glanced into the living room through the open doorway. There was one piece of yellow crime scene tape across the door. "And this is where Mr. Burris was killed last night?"

Sarah took a deep breath. "Yes. I don't think the sheriff

is really serious about me as a suspect. Maybe I'm wrong. What do you think?"

Steve stood beside his wife and surveyed the living room from behind the crime scene tape. "I'd have to talk to the sheriff to answer that, and I can't do that as a director for the FBI."

"She's not asking for your professional opinion." Peggy nudged him. "We're her friends. Should she get a lawyer?"

"If she's not guilty, she has nothing to hide."

She smiled at Sarah. "In other words, yes. Get a lawyer. Maybe you should call Hunter. I know that's what you do too, but always better to have a second opinion."

"Thanks. I guess you two have different ideas about how the law works, huh?"

"Even though my wife is surrounded by police officers that are her friends and family, she's always skeptical," Steve said.

"It's who I am." Peggy shrugged. "I think it may be part of being a scientist. We never trust anyone else's opinion. We have to do the work and form our own."

After their time in the house looking things over, Peggy and Steve headed back to their home in Charlotte. Sarah would have liked to have shown them the pumpkin patch and other parts of the farm that were visible. But neither one of them was dressed for a walk through the grass that lay fresh and wet on the ground. Sarah knew it stuck to everything until it dried.

Mr. Pope and his tractor were gone. She thought about going to his place and writing him a check, but she knew he wouldn't take it. She'd have to think of some other way to thank him, even though Jack had promised to help with the barn-raising. That wasn't her or a member of her family.

Exhausted and definitely feeling the need for a shower and clean clothes, Sarah headed back to her hotel. She'd only brought what she was wearing and the clothes she'd changed into. It was a long trip back to Richmond just to pick up other clothes. She opted to buy two new pairs of jeans and two tops. She washed what she'd been wearing that day and stopped to put her suit in at a local dry cleaner.

The look on the man's face when he saw her torn and puckered navy suit was priceless.

"We could do some repair work on this, if you like," he offered.

"That would be great, but I'm only in town for a few days."

"Twenty-four hour service." He pointed to his sign at the window. "Come back tomorrow. It'll be done. Thank you for your business."

She'd put off the phone calls until lunch. At that point, she used the phone in the hotel room to call her boss. Clare Rosemond had been in the state senate for more than twenty years. She was a good boss and a good friend. Sarah knew she'd understand her predicament.

"Just how serious is this local sheriff about you killing the man you were supposed to meet?" Clare asked. "I don't mind you having a few extra days off, especially since you're only a phone call away. But do you need help? I can have an excellent lawyer down there today."

Sarah laughed. "So you've been talking to another lawyer while I've been gone? I thought I was the best lawyer you knew."

"You're so crazy. You can't defend yourself properly. Really, do you need some help?"

"I'm fine right now. If that changes, I'll let you know."

"What about this mountain man living on your property? That sounds exciting. What does he look like?"

"He looks like the beast in *Beauty and the Beast*," Sarah said. They'd gone to see the Broadway play together a few months before.

"We know how that turned out for Belle," Clare reminded her. "What do you think about him? Do you think he killed this reporter to keep you from finding the truth about your grandparents?"

Sarah really didn't think so, though it would've been

easy to say yes. He might live somewhere on the property, and never changed clothes, but everyone loved him, including her grandparents. Maybe his personal issues had kept him from getting back out in the world. She already knew he'd had a troubled childhood. But that didn't make him a killer.

She suspected that he knew something more about her grandparents' disappearance than he was admitting, but she didn't think he was responsible for it.

"I don't know what to think about him," she said. "But I don't have to make that decision. I already have an offer on the farm. I wasn't able to take advantage of it after everything that happened, but I'm meeting with the real estate agent and the buyer later today."

"That sounds like good news anyway."

"I think so."

"You have some reservation about selling the property?" Clare asked. "What changed your mind? You were gung ho about it before you left here."

"I don't know." Three new messages popped up on her cell phone as she was talking. "I have to go. I'll call again later. If you need anything, you can call me."

"Okay. Take care of yourself. Let me know if you need any help. See you later."

Sarah returned Mace's call. If she thought he seemed anxious earlier, he was almost distraught when he spoke to her.

"I've been trying to get in touch with you," he said. "Where have you been? You know this deal won't last forever, right?"

His level of panic took her by surprise. "I'm sorry, but I had some things I had to take care of."

"Are you serious about selling the property or not?"

"Of course I'm serious," she assured him.

"Because a buyer like this won't come around again."

She took a deep breath. With little sleep the night before, and too many questions on her mind, her reply was more impatient than it would have otherwise been. “Maybe we should move on to the next buyer, Mace. I’m not in a big rush to sell. When it happens, it happens.”

“What? You don’t know what you’re saying. This is the deal of the century. Another buyer, if we could find one, would never be this motivated.”

Sarah could imagine him with smoke coming out of his ears and his eyes bulging.

“Who’s the buyer?” she asked. “What makes him so motivated?”

“Come to my office at one. He’ll be there, and we can sign the papers. Okay?”

“All right. That’s fine. I’ll be there. Thanks.”

She put down the phone and wondered what could possibly be so important about signing the papers that day. There had been no movement with the land for sixteen years. She couldn’t wait to meet the buyer and ask a few questions.

Chapter Six

Sarah was ready early and decided to grab some food to go. She wanted to take it out to the farm and look around a bit now that the grass wasn't such an obstacle. It might be the last time she could walk around the land while it was still hers.

The day was beautiful. There were farmers out working from Suffolk to Misty River. Some of the crops she could identify—corn, wheat, hay. Others she had no idea. But it was interesting watching as it was harvested. Huge pieces of machinery had replaced the old hand-cutting methods. She could remember her grandfather waving to her from his tractor as he went out to cut down the cornstalks.

Some of her friends from Richmond would be surprised to find out what a country girl she was at heart. Those years spending time with her grandparents had shaped her more than she'd thought. It wasn't that she wanted to be a farmer exactly. It was more that she had a distinct appreciation for the land and the work that was done on it.

Her mother had never felt anything but stifled by the place she was born. She'd obviously passed that on to Sarah's brother, Dusty. Since their mother understood how terrible it was, she rarely made him visit. For Sarah, it had been like having her own grandparents that she didn't have to share.

She parked the rental car at the end of the drive and grabbed the white bag with her sandwich, chips, and sweet tea before she started walking around the house.

It was easy to see the barn now. She found the old spring house and various other outbuildings where crops were stored or animals were kept. She sat in the sun near the pumpkin patch and the barn with the sweet smell of grass and the pleasant droning of bees around her.

There was a mother cat nursing her six black and white babies. She didn't run off as Sarah had expected. Instead she licked her paws and cleaned her babies, at ease with a human so close. Maybe she belonged to Jack.

Sarah would never forget this place. The magic she'd felt as a child still lived in her when she looked at it. Some things never changed, even though her heart still ached with not being able to find her grandparents. The memories of so many happy times here would always be a part of her.

Because she was tired and a little depressed from not finding answers, she lay back on the sweet-smelling grass and closed her eyes. She knew she'd have grass in her hair and maybe some dirt on her jeans, but it was worth that moment of peace.

She smiled, remembering how she'd done the same thing as a child and then opened her eyes.

"I didn't expect to find you here." Jack was leaning over her.

She sat up quickly, feeling defensive after he'd found her relaxing in the sun by the cats. "It doesn't surprise me to find you here at all."

"You don't sound too pleased by it."

"Thanks for having the grass cut. But you don't have to help put up the barn for Mr. Pope. I'll pay him for his work."

He sat beside her on the grass and stroked the black and white cat. His hands were big but gentle. It reminded Sarah of what Mr. Pope had said about helping with the foals.

"It's always a big party—the barn-raising. Lots of potato salad, fried chicken, and banana pudding. I'd go whether he cut the grass or not. He knows it. We call that being good neighbors."

"That's fine." She shifted away from him and the cats. "At least with the grass cut, I can figure out where you've been hiding."

"There's not much to figure. I've lived in the barn for years."

"With the cat, I'm guessing."

"For now." He smiled as the cat arched her back under his caress.

"Why not the house?" she asked curiously. "You knew it was empty. You would've been more comfortable there."

He played with a piece of long grass between his fingers. "I don't know. It didn't seem right. What would I have said if Tommy came home and I was living in his house?"

"You still think they'll come home? It's been a long time."

"They never gave up on me. I won't give up on them."

She watched him closely. "I got a good offer to sell the farm. I'm meeting with the buyer at one."

"Sounds great—if you're sure that's what you want."

"What do you mean? It's the only reason I came here. Of course I want to sell. My family is depending on me to take care of it."

"I didn't mean anything by it, Sarah. But you're the only member of your family who ever wanted to spend time here."

"My life is in Richmond," she debated, though she knew she didn't have to. She didn't have to defend her decisions to him. "The sooner I get back where I belong, the better."

"I guess you have it all worked out." He got to his feet in

a single lithe movement. "Have you been down by the river yet?"

"You should know. You follow me around."

He held out his hand. "You remember swimming there when you were a kid?"

She smiled. "Yes. Is the old tree swing still there?"

"Let's go see."

Sarah gave him her hand, and he helped her to her feet. "Thanks."

"Sure. Want to go by the barn and take a look at my place so you've seen it all?"

"No. I don't think so. Just the river, please." She remembered that sweet childish kiss they'd shared. It made her uncomfortable, though he'd probably forgotten it a long time ago. She put both her hands in her pockets. "I'd almost forgotten about the river."

"That's because you couldn't find it until the grass was cut." He led the way down a well-worn path.

"I think I could've found it. I was down there enough as a kid. Did you swim there?"

"Of course. There was nothing like it after a hot day working. Still isn't."

She followed him down the narrow trail that led through the trees to the edge of the river. The oaks were heavy with green leaves that were just starting to change to gold and red. The scent of the pines was pleasant in the hot sun. Large pine cones hung from their boughs.

"You know, this property has the longest river frontage in the county. People have started using the river for canoeing and other watersports the last few years."

"What about all the rocks?" One of the things she'd loved about the river was the rocks that stuck out of the shallow water. She'd climbed across them, going from bank to bank many times. Sometimes in the spring there was flooding. Otherwise it was a perfect place to swim and play.

"They don't seem to mind the rocks," he said.

Sarah saw the river as they came around the last of the

heavy forest that protected it. It was as she remembered—even the thick rope swing with two knots in it was still there.

"This is exactly like I remember." She gave the rope a tug. "I don't know how I ever managed to swing out on this and drop into the water without killing myself."

"It's the big pool in the middle." He pointed toward the only deep water between the smooth gray rocks. "Did you know there's a county marker in the middle of the river? It's been there since the county was first mapped in the early 1800s."

"No." She couldn't believe there was anything here she'd missed. "Where?"

"Follow me." He grinned and started walking along the riverbank.

Sarah followed on the brown mud. Her new boots would never be the same, but she kept her jeans clean by rolling up the cuffs.

"How did you find it?" she asked.

"Surveyors. Everyone has been looking at the county boundaries to make sure they're getting their fair share of taxes."

"Which side are we on?"

"We're still in the same county. Nothing in Misty River changed. The line moved between the counties a few miles down from here on the highway, but we weren't involved."

Jack pointed to a massive boulder in the middle of the river. Water tumbled around it creating mini falls on each side.

"It's right there on the other side of the big rock," he told her. "You have to go out there to see it."

She frowned. "You could've mentioned that. Falling in the water trying to see the county marker wouldn't be a good thing right now."

"That's probably true. I didn't think about that part since I wasn't worried about falling in."

Sarah looked again, wanting to see the marker. She might never be here again. "Okay. I'm not as sure-footed as I used to be, but I can probably stay out of the water. You go first. If you fall in, I'll go a different way."

He agreed and started across the rocks that made a bridge to the boulder. His long legs made it look easy to jump from stone to stone, going around the side of the small waterfall.

"Come on," he called. "Or did you just want me to take a picture for you?"

"No. I'm coming." She started out on the first rock and reached the second easily enough to feel more confident in the adventure. She wasn't sure why she wanted to see an old county marker in the river, but it appealed to that little girl in her soul that had never turned down a challenge.

Sarah reached the spot where she had to jump across the waterfall beside the boulder. She managed to clear it, but getting around the massive rock was difficult.

"Here." He put out his hand. "Let me help you."

She grabbed his warm hand and got halfway across the gray rock before she lost her balance and dropped into the pool that was fed by the dual waterfalls. She came up sputtering, forgetting how cold the river was except in the heat of summer. It wasn't deep—her feet touched the bottom. River water ran off her clothes.

"Don't you dare laugh," she warned him.

"What? You actually found the perfect spot to view the county marker. Look right here."

There was a three-foot stone that stuck straight out of the dark water. A county name was etched into the sides that faced each river bank as well as the name of the original surveyor and the date.

"Wow. I can't believe I missed that after all the times I walked up and down these banks."

As she said it, her cell phone fell out of her pocket into the swirling water.

"Pick it up," he said. "You can put it in rice and dry it out."

She retrieved the phone even though she was doubtful

about his idea. Shoving it in her pocket, she climbed back on the rocks to get out of the river. There was no way she was going to make her appointment with Mace and his buyer if she had to go back to the hotel and change. She knew before she made the call that her real estate agent might have a heart attack if she had to put it off again.

"Too bad about your appointment." A smile played over his lips.

Sarah waited for him to join her on the bank. "You did this on purpose, didn't you? It's your way of trying to stop the sale. I get it. You don't want to leave."

"I didn't push you in the water."

"Well, don't worry. I'll figure something out." Her teeth were chattering even though the day was warm.

"Sounds like you need to get out of those clothes." Even though he didn't smile, his blue eyes were amused at her discomfort.

"Sure. I bet you'd like that, wouldn't you? Maybe we should go back to the barn and both take off our clothes."

"I'm game if you are."

"It would have to be a lot colder than this." She stormed up from the edge of the water and followed the path through the trees away from the woods. Moving quickly made her warmer. But her clothes were still full of water, and her boots squished.

She glanced back, halfway across the field past the spring house. There was no sign of Jack. Maybe he took off his clothes and built a fire, hoping she'd return. The man had a lot of nerve for someone who looked like he never bathed and lived in a barn.

Sarah had an idea and let herself in the house. She went upstairs to her mother's old room, dripping along the way. Her grandparents had always kept it as it had been when she'd moved out. Sarah had slept in that room when she visited. She'd spent a lot of time looking through the old clothes in the closet. There might be something there that she could wear, at least for the meeting.

As she went upstairs, she noticed that the house was a little dusty but not what she'd expect after sixteen years. Jack wasn't staying in here, but he'd been knocking down cobwebs and keeping up with things. The floors were clean, and the lights hanging from the ceiling had working lightbulbs in them.

Lucky for her, she and her mother were about the same size. Her mother was shorter but that didn't matter to the black and white dress Sarah pulled out of the cedar chest. She even found underwear and a bra. Her mother still had packrat tendencies—she had to force herself to throw anything away. In this case, it was a good thing.

The dress was okay, if a little short. It was better than her wet clothes. The black shoes she found pinched her toes—her mother's feet were a size smaller. But it would do for her appointment. She dried her hair and combed it straight back away from her face.

She looked unusual, but she'd do, Sarah decided with a quick glance at herself in the full-length mirror on the back of the bedroom door.

There wasn't any time to waste. She ran back down the stairs and left for the real estate office. She thought about the rice trick Jack had mentioned but didn't have any rice to try it. She had a maintenance plan on her phone, but she'd have to go to Suffolk to figure that out. If anyone called, they'd have to wait for updates on what she was doing.

Mace was pacing his small office, one of the few buildings at the crossroads of the two highways that had created Misty River. "I was beginning to worry that you weren't coming, Ms. Tucker."

Sarah could hear the sigh of relief in his voice as he shook her hand.

"Sorry," she said. "I had an accident, and it took longer to get here than I thought."

"I hope it wasn't anything serious." A man possibly in his early forties came out of a side room. He was well-dressed, with black, close-cut hair and a winning smile. "I'm

Leland Drake. Let's do this thing and make some money."

Chapter Seven

They sat down together at a table by a window that looked out at the parking lot. Dozens of large trucks whizzed by on both highways, going quickly through the intersection, barely noticing the small community. There was a green sign at both sides of the intersection that proudly proclaimed *Misty River* but no population number since the town was unincorporated.

Sarah accepted a cup of coffee from Mace. It was terrible, but at least it was warm. Her hands were still cold from the river.

"I understand how I'm going to make money," she said to Leland since he'd brought it up. "How are you going to make money?"

"I'll be happy to share. May I call you Sarah? I feel like I know you. I knew your family years ago."

"Sure."

He rubbed his hands together. "Your property is pivotal

to my plans. You have the longest river frontage in the county. A new, state-wide Blue Way is in the works. It includes two spots on Misty River. One of them will be on your land—my land—complete with a general store where canoers can purchase what they need. The other spot on the river is on my family's property near the county line."

Sarah understood why Jack had taken her to the river. She wasn't sure what he'd hoped to gain unless it was trying to get her to feel nostalgic before she learned about the plans for the farm.

Misty River was as famous for its gossip as any other small town. She wasn't hooked into it because she didn't live there. Jack knew because he heard everything.

Part of her had been hoping that some family wanted the farm because they wanted to live there and raise a family as her grandparents and great-grandparents had. It wasn't practical, not in this day and age, despite what Mr. Pope had said. She felt sad that no other little girl would visit her family there and experience all the joys she had. On the other hand, at least Leland didn't want to build condos. She was going to have to take what good she could from this.

"I have the contracts ready right here." Mace's lawyer put out three sets of papers and gave each of them a pen with the name of his real estate company on it. "Whenever you're ready, read through everything. I marked the spaces where you should sign beside your typed names. Then we can all go home happy."

"What about the property being the scene of a crime?" Sarah felt she should ask to be honest about the circumstances.

"Not to worry," the lawyer told her. "Since the buyer has been apprised of the situation, we can go ahead with the deal."

She was happy that it would be over. She pushed aside her feeling of sadness and loss. The chances were good that Jack was wrong. Wherever her grandparents had gone, they weren't coming back. She couldn't stay here to look for them. She had to sign the papers, get her things together, and go home. She could always give the sheriff her information in Richmond if there was anything else he needed to know about Mr. Burris's death.

"If you see anything that bothers you." Mace was watching her. "Just let me know. We can move things around if you need more time."

"But not much more." Leland winked at her. "I have to get this on the county schedule as soon as possible to be eligible for the available grant money."

"I understand." She glanced through the paperwork. It was what she'd expected as far as terms were concerned. "I think this will be a great project for Misty River. It shows growth potential."

"Exactly what I was thinking." Leland smiled. "I didn't expect to see anyone from your family. How are they doing up in Richmond?"

"Everyone is fine, thanks." No doubt he was the one Mace had spoken of when he said someone had wanted to pay the back taxes and get the land that way.

The front door of the building opened, and a man in jeans and a red plaid shirt glanced around, removing his straw hat.

"Can I help you?" Mace raced to the door to stop the land sale from being interrupted.

"Yeah." The man in red plaid nodded to Sarah and Leland. "I have a court injunction that's been filed with the county to stop the sale of Elizabeth and Thomas Denning's property. Maybe you should take a look at it before you go any farther."

The man was clearly ill-at-ease being there. That made Sarah curious. Before he could hand the injunction to Mace, she took it and quickly read the document.

"This is crazy." She looked at the newcomer. "Why are you doing this?"

"Excuse me, ma'am." The man in red plaid reached to shake her hand. "I'm Trent Waddington. I filed this injunction on behalf of my client, who prefers to remain anonymous."

Sarah shook his hand. "My grandparents have been missing for much longer than the requisite seven years needed to take over their business affairs as appointed by their sole surviving heir, my mother."

"That's true," Trent agreed. "But there's the little matter of your grandparents actually being declared legally dead by the state. I couldn't find a record of that, Ms. Tucker. If you have the paperwork, we can take care of that right now."

"Excuse me a moment." Sarah asked to use Mace's phone in his side office.

She called her mother and asked about the formality that was holding up the deal.

"I'm sure we filed that at the seven-year mark," her mother said while she spoke to someone in her office. "Let me check that out and get back with you."

"Quickly, please. I'm standing here with the contract and the buyer."

"I'll put Suzi on it right away. I should have an answer in the next five minutes."

Sarah put down the phone when her mother hung up. Suzi was her personal assistant. Surely the paperwork had been filed.

She wondered about the anonymous client Trent was talking about, and an image formed in her mind. No doubt it was Jack trying to stop the sale at the last minute. But where would he come up with the money to hire a lawyer?

"Probably offered to build his barn or something," she muttered to herself.

Mace tapped at the door and came into the room. "Well? Is there really a legal issue that's preventing you from selling the farm?"

"I don't know yet," she admitted. "My mother should've been the one to file that paperwork. She'll get back to me as soon as she can."

He glanced toward the open room. "We could lose this

sale, you know. Leland wants the property, but he won't wait forever."

"I know. He wants it in time to get his money back in grants. But on the other hand, if this is only one of two spots on the river that can be used for the Blue Way, I think he'll be a little patient while we check into this."

"I certainly hope so," he said tartly before he left the small office.

It only took another minute for the phone to ring. It was Suzi with bad news. "I'm sorry, Ms. Tucker. It appears as though that paperwork you requested was never filed. I'll take care of it right away."

"Put my mother on the phone," Sarah demanded.

"She's very busy. Maybe you could call her later."

"No. Put her on the phone now, please."

There was a brief pause, and then Sarah's mother answered. "I'm so sorry, honey. I guess I got caught up in other things and forgot to file. It will only take a few days. This is Thursday. You should have it back by Monday. You said the police chief told you not to leave for a day or so. Get through the weekend. Hopefully everything will be fine by then."

"You could've checked this before you sent me down here."

"I know. You have a right to be angry. It just slipped my mind. I'm sorry. I'll talk to you later."

Sarah put the heavy yellow phone receiver back down on the cradle. She was furious, but there was nothing she could do but wait. She could go back to Richmond for the weekend and come back Monday, if the paperwork was filed. Maybe that's what she'd do.

She put on a tight smile as she walked out of the office to face the three men.

"It appears as though some mistakes were made, gentlemen. However, these are mistakes that can be easily rectified. The paperwork regarding my grandparents' death will be filed today. We'll have to wait until Monday to finish the transaction. I apologize."

Leland brought his fist down on the table. "Is this some kind of ploy to get more money for the property?"

"I assure you it's not." She remained calm even in the face of his temper. She'd dealt with plenty of angry clients.

"This is unacceptable," Mace blustered. "Leland has the right to withdraw his offer on the property."

Sarah picked up her bag. "Of course that choice is his. As soon as I hear that the documents are ready, I'll let you know. I apologize again for this unfortunate situation."

"Wait!" Leland grabbed Mace by the sleeve. "She's not leaving, is she?"

"There's more we should be talking about," Mace yelped.

"Really, there isn't anything else at this juncture," she replied. "I'll be in touch."

But she grabbed Trent as she was walking out the front door and pinned him against the brick wall outside the building.

"Jack put you up to this, didn't he?" she asked. "What did he offer to trade if you did this for him?"

"I don't know what you're talking about," he said nervously. "I was only doing my job."

"Representing who?"

"Not representing anyone." He smiled and played with his clip-on tie. "I'm not a lawyer. Not really. I'm a legal aid. Jack asked me to see if Mr. and Mrs. Denning had been declared legally dead. They weren't. I told you before you sold the property. You didn't want to sell it if everything wasn't right, did you?"

"No." She let him go—not that he couldn't have gotten away if he'd wanted to. She'd pressed her hand against his chest, but he was at least six inches taller than her and much broader. "Why doesn't he just get with the program? I'm going to sell this land."

Trent shrugged. "I don't know. You should ask him. I have to get back to work. Have a nice day."

Sarah wasn't sure what to do. Jack had a target painted on his head as far as she was concerned. He let her walk into this—after a dunk in the river. She wanted to hit him with something.

She went back to the farm and yelled his name a few times. There was no answer from the acres that stretched in front of her. He only showed up when he wanted to. She reached down to stroke the black and white mother cat as her babies scurried along behind her.

"Fine." She wished she had a microphone. "Stay out there, but stop interfering. We're going to sell this farm. Get used to it. Find another place to live."

Sheriff Morgan pulled up in the drive when she was about to get back in her car.

"I heard about your bad news," he said with a smile. "Grace told me down at the Quik-Chek. Word travels fast. A family of lawyers and no one thought to file the paperwork declaring your grandparents legally dead. I'd call that a travesty of justice, ma'am."

"Is there some reason for your visit?" she asked. "Or did Jack hire you to bully me?"

That brought a rich chuckle from him. "That Jack gets around pretty good for a man who doesn't have a car."

Sarah seethed. "Sheriff?"

"Sorry. Just ribbing you some." He reached through the window of his car and brought out the file that she'd given him. "George Burris was a good man, Ms. Tucker, but I'm not sure what this information had to do with your grandparents' disappearance. Did you look at it?"

"Not much. Jack sneaked it out of the kitchen, remember?" She took the file from him. It must be completely unimportant since it could be evidence in a murder case and he was giving it back. "You don't think Mr. Burris was killed for this?"

"Nope. Not considering the killer left it behind. Take a look. Give me a call if you have any questions. I hear you'll be here until at least Monday. I don't know if George's death will be wrapped up that neatly. But I'm sure you'll give me your contact info if you decide to go back to Richmond."

"Thanks. I'll let you know."

He grinned. "Good thing you have a phone at the hotel, huh? Grace said your phone went for a swim."

"You could say that. I'll talk to you later, Sheriff Morgan."

"That Jack. He really cracks me up."

Chapter Eight

Sarah ignored her irritation with Jack and Sheriff Morgan and drove back to the hotel. Her boots were ruined. She went out and bought a new pair. She washed clothes again and picked up her suit at the dry cleaners. There wasn't much they could do with it. Sarah was pretty sure she'd never wear it again.

After taking a shower and changing clothes, she lay down on the bed and opened the folder George Burris had wanted her to see.

It was full of pictures, most black and white, some in color. Some were very old. There were newspaper clippings from as far back as 1897. Many of the newer articles were by George. All of his information pertained to a lost chest of gold that had supposedly belonged to the Confederate Army.

Many of the articles were of the opinion that the South could have won the war if that gold wouldn't have gone missing. The whole thing was about people looking for the gold and believing it was somewhere on her grandparents' property.

Sarah muttered a few "crazies" and got up to get a Coke from the mini-fridge. She shifted to the brown chair by the door and started reading again.

Somehow an ancestor of hers, Big Mike Denning, had been credited—or accused, depending on what side of the war you were on—of stealing the gold. Many people thought he'd taken it to end the war. George and some of his friends believed the gold was still there on the farm. There were maps, supposedly drawn by Big Mike himself. But the gold still remained unfound.

The hotel phone rang. It was Hunter wanting to know how everything was going and if she'd sold the property. "And where's your cell phone? I tried calling you a few times and left messages. What's up?"

"It's been a much bigger adventure than I'd expected." She told Hunter about George Burris, her wet cell phone, and then described the catastrophe trying to finalize the sale of the land. "I can't tell you how embarrassing it was to be outmaneuvered by a man who lives on my land illegally."

Hunter laughed at her. "I'm not sure if your mom really wants to sell the place or not. It seems like she's ignored it, but I think she's got doubts."

Sarah agreed. "I was just looking at the file that Mr. Burris died trying to show me. It doesn't make any sense. It's all pictures of my grandparents and articles about looking for lost gold on their property. Even the sheriff didn't want it."

"Treasure hunting? Does the sheriff think Mr. Burris was killed for that?"

"He's not exactly the sharing type, although he gave me the file he had on my grandparents' disappearance. It's skimpy, Hunter. And he hasn't offered any ideas on why the man was killed at the house. He makes me feel like he thinks I'm a suspect, but Jack thinks that's stupid."

"Jack, huh?" Hunter asked. "Have you actually been charged with anything?"

"No. I guess it might be like a person of interest thing. The sheriff gave me this information, but he still has my gun."

"Probably checking ballistics. Do you want me to come back up? I can be there in a few hours. I don't like that you're there alone."

"I thought about going home for the weekend," Sarah admitted. "But I can't get involved with anything there until I can clear this up. I guess I'll just stay here until Monday."

"What about this man who's hanging around your farm? You said the sheriff didn't question him about Mr. Burris's death."

"Not as far as I know," Sarah said. "Jack was right there with me when the first shot was fired. I don't think he was responsible for it, even though he's incredibly annoying. But I don't know for sure. It could be some elaborate set up."

"You could probably get a no-trespassing warrant against him," Hunter told her. "If he's squatting out there, I'm sure the sheriff would get him off if you pressed it."

Sarah looked at her freckles in the hotel room mirror. "I know. But I feel sorry for him. I don't know what happened to him, but he thinks he's protecting the property for my grandparents. He thinks they're coming back."

"That sounds like a problem. And the sheriff doesn't think Jack had anything to do with your grandparents disappearing either?"

"No. He's just good old Jack. It's a weird situation. My mother should've kept up with what was going on out there all these years—or sold the place. This is so unlike her. She doesn't usually ignore problems or have butter fingers. You might be right about how she really feels."

"I'd be careful out there anyway. This guy might seem harmless, but you don't know that he didn't kill your grandparents in his search for the gold and then take out Mr. Burris because he knew about it."

"I'm probably not going out there again until Monday. I'll get a new phone and catch up on some work with my laptop here at the hotel. It's lucky that I can work from anywhere."

"Just watch your back," Hunter said. "The whole thing sounds kind of scary."

"Thanks. I will." Sarah wanted to tell her friend about the teenage Jack that she remembered, and that first awkward kiss. But she didn't mention it. She didn't want her friend to give up her weekend to come to her rescue.

There was a coffee shop close to the hotel. Sarah was ready to get out of the room for a while.

She ran a comb through her hair. It didn't seem to like the time she'd spent outdoors or the dip in the river. It was standing up all over. She twisted it into place and secured it on the back of her head.

Her skin was pink from the extra sun, and she swore she had a few more freckles than she'd started out with. She wanted to go home and leave all of this for Dusty or her mother. It was turning out to be a lot more than she'd thought it would.

But she had to see it through. It had to be done right this time.

She was going to get a replacement for her wet phone first, she decided. Then she could sit at the coffee shop and take a look at it. She thought about what Jack had suggested about putting the phone in rice. If the idea had come from anyone else, she might try it. At that moment, she wanted to put Jack in rice.

It was a strange, naked feeling not having her phone with her. She felt out of touch and frequently stuck her hand in her pocket or handbag to check it, only to find it wasn't there. Funny how people had grown so dependent on them. She couldn't wait to get hers back.

The surprisingly friendly clerk moved her information from her data card to another phone. Sarah was glad she frequently backed up her pictures and other important items. New phone in hand, she went to the coffee shop only to find a dozen messages from various people. Her mother had left several messages, and so had Clare. Sheriff Morgan had left the most recent message.

Sarah got a mocha latte from a good-looking barista who flirted with her by licking whipped cream from his finger as he gazed into her eyes. She was smiling on her way to the table as she returned the sheriff's call.

"Looks like we're not gonna luck out and find the rifle that was used to kill George. We got a tip that it was hidden in some brambles on your property, but there was nothing but some shell casings and candy wrappers. We got a few smudged prints off that stuff. I was wondering if you might consider coming out here and giving us a few fresh prints."

"My fingerprints? Seriously?" Her voice got loud in her frustration, and people at a nearby table stared at her. She lowered her tone. "So I'm actually a suspect?"

"It's mostly just to rule out your prints from the ones we found, create a baseline of people we know were there. We're having some difficulty getting a copy of your prints from Senator Rosemond's office in Richmond. They should be on file, but we're getting stonewalled. I can't make you do this, Ms. Tucker, but it could help us out. We both want the same thing, right?"

"My prints aren't on any candy wrappers or shell casings you found on the property, Sheriff Morgan." She took a deep breath to get a handle on her irritation. "But I'll be glad to come out and be printed if that will help."

"That would be a big help," he replied. "We're going to dust for prints in the house too. Maybe we'll get lucky and find the same prints in there that are on the shell-casings."

Remembering the weapon Jack had described from the sound the shot had made, Sarah asked, "Do you have a ballistics report yet, Sheriff?"

"I do," he agreed. "The weapon that killed George was a Ruger 77/357. It's a specialty rifle."

"It has a loud report," she returned. "Jack said that's what it sounded like."

"Guess he'd know. I'll see you when you get here."

Sarah got in her car after finishing her coffee and sat at the wheel for a few minutes before starting it. Her hands trembled on the steering wheel. The situation was beginning to scare her. How had Jack known what rifle Mr. Burris was shot with? She'd told the sheriff what he said, why didn't he think of him as a potentially dangerous suspect?

She didn't know what to do. What if Jack came after her next because she still planned to sell the land?

Calm down. Take a deep breath.

As far as she knew, Jack didn't drive. If she couldn't convince the sheriff to question him about Mr. Burris's death, she could at least stay away from him. Maybe she could find another way to come at this problem with Jack and Sheriff Morgan being buddies. There were always other law enforcement agencies to consult with, right? With a new perspective on the matter, Sarah started the car and drove toward the sheriff's office, following the directions from her GPS.

The building was red brick with a flat, tarred roof. There were dozens of brown sheriff's cars parked around it with dozens more civilian cars. She grabbed her bag and looked at her reflection in the rearview mirror.

"You haven't done anything wrong. You don't have to be nervous about going in there."

But the words didn't comfort her. She still had butterflies in her stomach. She forced herself out of the car and into the office. People were waiting in the dozen or so straight-back, wood chairs in front of a big counter. Behind the counter were desks and county sheriff personnel.

Before she could take a seat, Sheriff Morgan saw her and personally escorted her to the other side of the counter. He showed her to a seat in a small interrogation room and offered to get her some coffee. Sarah stared at a pair of handcuffs that were on the table next to her.

They aren't for you.

"Thank you for coming in, Ms. Tucker." He returned with another woman in uniform. "Dee Dee will take your prints, and then we'll talk, okay?"

He was still just as friendly as he had been before he was looking for her fingerprints. Maybe he really was just ruling her out as a suspect. Maybe he didn't think she was guilty of anything.

Dee Dee was nice too. She was very gentle as she carefully put each finger on the ink pad and then rolled them on a piece of paper with Sarah's name and social security number printed on the top.

"This is to clean your hands." Dee Dee gave her a wipe to get the ink off. "That's all there is to it. Just relax, and the sheriff will be right with you."

Sarah's hands were cold as she cleaned the ink. What was it about being here that made her so nervous? She'd had to go to police stations in Richmond all the time for various reasons. This was no different.

Jack should be down here too.

Sheriff Morgan returned. "Sorry about that, Ms. Tucker. I had to make sure everything was done that could be done. I don't like having a killer out there laughing at me. It doesn't give the people faith in their sheriff."

"I assume that means my fingerprints weren't on the casings or candy bar wrappers?" She held her breath. Of course they weren't there.

"No, ma'am. I didn't expect to find them, but like I said, just being thorough." He shrugged and sat opposite her at the table.

"I know I keep saying this—but what about Jack? Have you checked his fingerprints? He knew what kind of gun was fired at George. Doesn't that count for something?"

"As a matter of fact, it does. We know the two of you were there from your statements. I can't think of any reason you or Jack would kill George Burris, but sometimes people do strange things."

"So you had someone bring Jack down here and checked his fingerprints too?" She just wanted to make sure he understood what she was asking and it wasn't just a 'feeling' of his that Jack wasn't guilty.

"I get your point." He smiled. "But I didn't have to bring Jack in to check his prints. There was some chicken stealing going on a few years back, and people thought it might be him. The computer found his fingerprints in the military database. He wasn't the one stealing chickens, by the way. And I don't think he had anything to do with your grandparents' disappearance. He was in school that day, living with his father in the next county over."

"Oh."

"I know Jack and his prints. He didn't kill George Burris, but he does know his weaponry."

Apparently there were actual reasons why the sheriff trusted Jack. She'd thought it was more a blind trust the way he'd said it, but it seemed to be something else. What was it about him that everyone liked and trusted him so much? She couldn't see it.

"Let me ask you a thing or two. Did you notice anything when George was killed? I know you heard a shot that was loud. Jack said the two of you hit the dirt at that point. Then there was another shot."

She nodded. "And the glass broke. Jack had my gun and left me there to see what was going on. He told me not to get up. It was too dark to see anything except for the light in the living room. When he came back, we went into the house and found Mr. Burris on the floor with the file beside him."

Sheriff Morgan nodded as he doodled on some paper, not looking up at her. "Which was the file you gave me that held all the information about treasure hunting on your property—is that right?"

"As far as I know."

"Yeah. Jack has a thing about people coming out there wanting to dig holes on the land. I've found more than one trespasser tied to a tree. It's been a long time. I thought maybe that was all over. But I guess a legend about a trunk full of gold never goes away."

"Why is he staying there like some human guard dog?

No one is that faithful to a promise."

"I think you should ask him yourself." Sheriff Morgan got to his feet. "You're free to go, but like I said, leave your contact information in case we have any other questions."

"You already have it, and I'm not going anywhere." Her tone was surly.

He chuckled. "Thanks for coming in, Ms. Tucker."

Sarah left quickly, glad to be finished with that business. She didn't know what to make of Jack. He was either a crazy man or someone very dedicated to her grandparents. If she was lucky, she wouldn't see him again.

She checked her messages and found a text from her mother. Meet you at the farm tonight. Nine-thirty. Don't be late.

Why was she coming down from Richmond? Did she want to take over the sale of the property because she thought Sarah wasn't doing a good job?

Not looking forward to a visit from her mother, she stopped for gas at the Quik-Chek in Misty River. If the cashier knew everything that was going on, maybe she had information about Mr. Burris's death too.

Sarah was pumping gas when a rusted brown pickup pulled next to her.

A woman with sun-kissed brown hair stuck her head out the window. "Is that you, Sarah?"

"Yes." *What now?*

"It's me, Kathy Rankin. Remember? First time either of us went swimming naked in the river."

She couldn't have said anything else that would have made as much of an impact.

"Kathy!" Sarah called back. "I didn't know you were still living here."

"We can't all be big shot lawyers and move to Richmond." Kathy jumped out of the pickup and hugged her old friend. "I heard you were here and went over to the house a few times, but Jack said I just missed you each time. How are you? You look great!"

They had been best buddies when Sarah had come to visit as a child. Kathy's parents owned the large farm on the other side of her grandparents' property.

Swimming naked wasn't the only time they'd bent the rules. Sometimes they got caught and Kathy would be grounded from seeing Sarah for a while. Her parents thought Kathy was a bad influence too. But Sarah knew that most of the bad things they did together came from a combination of each other's imaginations.

"I'm fine. I suppose you know I'm selling the property."

"Of course I know. I wanted to buy it, but Mace said it was out of my league. He said Leland Drake was offering a fortune for it. I didn't bother going any further."

"I haven't signed the papers yet."

"I know. You forgot to have your grandparents declared legally dead." Kathy laughed. "What's up with that?"

"My mother thought she'd taken care of it." Sarah winced. "What about you? Still living on the farm with your parents?"

"Not exactly." Kathy sobered. "My mom died about five years ago. My dad last year. I inherited the farm since Mark doesn't like being outside, like Dusty never liked it. Is he still afraid of bees?"

Sarah laughed. Dusty had once encountered some bees in Kathy's yard—her family kept bees—and had run screaming all the way back to their grandparents' house.

"I don't know. I don't think he's ever outside except for the walk between the car and the apartment or his office. What about Mark?"

Mark was Kathy's younger brother. It was amazing how much the two boys were alike.

"He lives in Williamsburg. He does something with stocks and bonds. He's got one of those big fancy houses next to a country club. I don't see him much now that Dad is dead."

The gas pump had finished filling before they'd stopped talking. Sarah put the handle back on the pump and closed the gas cap on her car.

"Hey, let's have lunch," Kathy said. "Where are you staying?"

"In Suffolk, but that sounds great."

"We have to go to Burger Shack. Remember? It was always the last place we ate together before you had to leave. Let's go."

"Sounds good. Are the burgers and fries as greasy as ever?" Sarah laughed.

"You know it. Do you have to go inside?"

"I'm hoping to get some information from Grace, who seems to know everything around here. Go ahead. I'll catch up with you."

"She won't tell you anything. You're a stranger. Just a minute. I'll go in with you."

Kathy grabbed her handbag and left the pickup parked in the middle of the lot, blocking two lanes of traffic to the gas pumps.

Sarah laughed. Same old Kathy, but with a bigger toy than the go-cart they used to drive around as kids.

"You look great." Kathy's brown eyes flashed over Sarah. "No kids, huh? You look too skinny to have kids."

"No kids. You?"

"Nope. Not yet." Kathy grinned. "But I keep hoping."

"You look good too," Sarah complimented. "Are you still keeping horses? I remember when I was a kid thinking that every woman who rode horses was thin."

"You might be right." Kathy patted her flat stomach. "I heard once that a horse knows its weight limit and will throw you off if you're over it. I don't want that to happen."

They went inside the small convenience store. Grace was there bagging beer and cigarettes for a trucker. Her brown bouffant hair style was rigid with hairspray. She grinned and joked with the young truck driver.

"Let me do the talking." Kathy stepped in front of Sarah.

Sarah had never met Grace, but the woman was wearing a huge sparkly name tag that she couldn't miss on her red

Quik-Chek shirt. She didn't mind Kathy stepping up to talk to her. She wasn't sure what she was going to say in the first place.

"Hey, Grace." Kathy flashed her a smile. "Can I have some of that *Laffy-Taffy* over there? The banana kind. Thanks."

"Hey, sugar. How's that bean crop doing? I heard you lost most of it to those worms."

Sarah raised her brows. This woman really *did* know everything.

"You can't believe what you hear all the time," Kathy said. "But my friend, Sarah Tucker, was wondering what you've heard about old George Burris biting it at her house."

Grace stared at Sarah. "So you're the new girl, huh?"

"I suppose. But I'm not new. I've just been gone a while."

"That's right—the missing grandparents." Grace nodded sagely.

"Have you heard anything about that?" Kathy asked.

"Nope. Only what Jack has to say about it. But that's been a while."

"What about George Burris getting shot out there?" Kathy paid for her candy.

"I heard he was getting in the middle of something when he should've known better." Grace stared hard at Sarah. "He isn't the only one either. Better watch your back, new girl."

Chapter Nine

Even though Kathy and Sarah badgered the clerk for more information, Grace wouldn't say anything else. A large group of people came into the store, and the conversation was cut short.

"I wouldn't put too much stock into what she says anyway," Kathy disclaimed as the two women walked out of the store together.

"But she knows everything. She even knows about Jack."

"Everybody knows about Jack. Want to take my truck over to Burger Shack?"

"Sure. I'll leave my car on the side of the parking lot." Sarah got her keys. "What do you mean, everyone knows about Jack?"

Kathy picked her up and they went to the Burger Shack.

"Jack has been around for a while. You remember him from when we were kids, right? I had the biggest crush on him. You did too. He used to come out and help your grandparents," Kathy explained. "Now he keeps up your place."

"Except for cutting the grass, right?"

"Yeah. Except for that. Mr. Pope goes over it sometimes. I could bring my tractor, if you want."

"That's okay. Jack had Mr. Pope do it. Thanks."

"In case you didn't notice, your grandparents' house looks a lot like it did sixteen years ago. I could show you a few places around here that have been empty a lot less time and don't look nearly as good. He takes care of all the buildings and the pumpkin patch."

"I'm amazed at his long term dedication," Sarah said. "Do you think he expects me to pay him or something?"

"You've lived in the city too long, my friend." Kathy's eyes were sympathetic. "When my Dad was dying, I spent every minute at the hospital with him. The farm would've been a mess except for Jack and one of my men who took it on himself to make sure everything was okay. When I got home after Dad died, people had left me enough food to feed myself for a month. Jack and Ben had brought in the corn and taken care of the bees. I'd do it for Mr. Pope too or anyone else who needed it. Jack isn't so strange, except from your point of view."

Sarah still wasn't convinced, but it helped that her friend thought well of him.

"I heard people are looking for that gold again at your place," Kathy said. "Crazy, huh?"

"I was thinking about that," Sarah replied. "We barely heard about it from Grampa. He told us about Big Mike Denning, but I guess he didn't think the treasure was still there. At least he never looked for it that I know of."

Kathy laughed as she pulled into the parking lot at Burger Shack. "I'm sure we would've found it if it was there."

"I'm sure you're right." Sarah glanced around as she got out. "This place looks exactly the same. Is Jack keeping this up too?"

"No. But being the only restaurant out here keeps this place going. Come on. A chocolate milkshake is calling my name."

Even the pictures on the walls were the same ones Sarah remembered. The only thing that was different was the original owner's son had taken over after his death. Their pictures were on the wall.

Sarah ordered a cheeseburger, fries, and a Coke. Kathy got the same but with a shake. They sat next to the jukebox—the music was still from the 1960s. They'd joked about how old it was, even when they were kids.

A waitress brought out their meals and talked to Kathy for a while. She was the great-granddaughter of the original owner and was working her way through college with a scholarship. She wanted to be a neurosurgeon.

After the young waitress had gone back to the kitchen, Kathy asked Sarah about men in her life. It was the first time Sarah had the opportunity to say her divorce was final.

"Sounds like he was a dream." Kathy swirled her fry in catsup. "Maybe you gave up on him too fast."

"I don't think so. He gave up on me too." Sarah sipped her Coke. "What about you? Are you married?"

"No. Still waiting for the right person to ask, I guess. I've had a few people pop the question, but I couldn't imagine living with them. I've had my eye on someone for a while, but he hasn't noticed yet. I keep hoping he'll catch me staring at his butt one day and get the idea."

Sarah laughed at that. "Well that's one way!"

"Going to the barn-raising tomorrow at the Pope house?"

"Is it a social thing?"

"Of course. We take any opportunity—you know that! You can meet the man I hope to claim as my boy toy."

Thinking that she owed Mr. Pope anyway, Sarah agreed. "I'll be there for it. Maybe you can find a casual fling for me too!"

"No problem. I'm the best at finding men who want to

have a good time but not stick around too long."

They lingered over their food until most of the burger restaurant was empty between lunch and dinner. Kathy drove Sarah back to her car in time to find Deputy Ron Broadwell looking at the license plate on the back. He'd been the officer who'd flirted with Sarah after George had been killed.

"Uh-oh," Kathy said. "Looks like you've got some sweet talking to do. Invite him to the barn-raising. That'll keep him from giving you a ticket."

Sarah shook her head. "A ticket for what? I don't see any signs saying it's illegal to park here."

"He's probably sharpening his investigative skills," Kathy mocked. "Or he's already into you, and this is his way of asking you out."

"Yeah. I'm sure that's it." Sarah laughed as she grabbed her bag to get out of the truck. "No wonder you can't find anyone to date around here."

"We like our men strong, silent, and kind of stupid. See you later."

"It was great catching up with you. Now I have to find something to wear to the barn-raising."

"What? No jeans?"

On that note, Sarah got out and went to her car. She noticed that Kathy waited to see what was going on. She might only be nosey, but it was a nice gesture.

"Is something wrong, Deputy Broadwell?"

He glanced up with a frown between his eyes as though he hadn't noticed she was standing beside him. "Just checking out the abandoned vehicle."

"Not abandoned, Deputy. I left it here while I went to lunch."

"This isn't a public parking lot, Ms. Tucker. Maybe next time you should mention that you're leaving the vehicle to the clerk inside. That way she wouldn't have called me."

Sarah followed his nod toward the door where Grace was smoking a cigarette and watching them.

"I'm sorry. I didn't think about it." She smiled at him,

noticing his thick, reddish-brown hair and brown eyes. He had a deep dimple in his chin that gave him a boyish appearance. "Deputy Broadwell, are you going to the Pope's barn-raising tomorrow?"

He stretched away from the car to his full height, a few inches taller than her. "I might be out that way for a spell."

"Maybe you'd like to escort me. I wanted to thank you for your kindness after the murder. I don't know many people, and I'd hate to go alone."

He smiled and removed his hat. "I'd be happy to do that, ma'am, for a stranger in Misty River. What time would you like me to stop for you?"

"I'm not sure what time it starts, are you?"

"Probably daylight. We like to start on things early around here."

Daylight? Ugh. "That's fine. But maybe I should meet you there. I'll be coming from Suffolk."

"I'll look out for you, ma'am."

"Sarah." She reminded him, seeing Kathy in her pickup holding two thumbs up.

"Sure, Sarah." He put out his hand, cradling hers in it. "I'm Ron. I'll see you then."

She watched him walk away, wondering if Kathy was watching his butt as he got in his car. Why not go with him? She might as well have a little fun while she was here.

Kathy had always been good at pointing out the fun things in life. Sarah had missed that the last few years, knowing her marriage was ending and purposely keeping her head down. Maybe this was a good opportunity to break out of her rut.

She waved to her friend as she pulled the rental car out of the parking lot. She had an idea about taking some of the big pumpkins to the barn-raising. Maybe it was stupid. She wasn't sure. But Mr. Pope could give them to his helpers for coming out.

She drove back to the farm and frowned at the pumpkin patch sign again. If she was going to be here any longer, she'd have to fix that thing. Seeing it hanging down that way was driving her crazy.

Jack wasn't around. She went back in the house and rummaged through her mother's closet again until she found a pair of jeans and a T-shirt. They were a little big, so she wrapped a belt around her waist. There weren't any boots, but she found an old pair of tennis shoes that fit. This way she didn't have to drive back to the hotel and come back again to meet her mother. She could also check out the pumpkins and drag some back to the car. Maybe she could find a cart by the barn.

After Sheriff Morgan's more detailed explanation about Jack's life, she felt less nervous knowing he was out there somewhere. Maybe he really was just a Good Samaritan who felt he owed her grandparents a debt. At least she knew that the sheriff didn't trust him blindly—that made her feel better.

Despite everything, she liked the sheriff and thought he was trying to do a good job. With no other law enforcement in Misty River, he had a big responsibility patrolling the county and keeping up with the towns in it. She thought he was doing his best trying to catch George Burris's killer when he'd asked her to come in.

Knowing Jack lived in the barn made her tread carefully around it as she searched for a wagon or cart she could load pumpkins on. If she had to drag them one at a time to the car, she'd probably give up after only a few.

The barn was still in good condition, like the house. It needed a coat of paint, but Jack had apparently kept it up too. She heard the kittens calling for their mother as she looked around outside the structure. The door was closed. For all she knew, Jack was inside sleeping. She didn't want to disturb him.

But the kittens kept calling. The mother cat was at her feet, rubbing her head against Sarah's leg. With the door closed, maybe the cat couldn't get in to be with them. Sarah stood on her tiptoes to peek in the dirty window, but she couldn't see anything.

"I guess you really need to get in there, don't you?" She stroked the cat's fur.

The cat meowed back at her and began rubbing her head against the closed door. Sarah carefully opened it just an inch or so to let her in.

"I thought you said you didn't want to see my place," Jack said from behind her.

She jumped, and that made her angry. "Do you always have to creep up on me like that?"

"No." He smiled. "It's just fun watching you jump."

"I'm glad you were entertained." She slammed the barn door closed. "I was just letting the cat in to be with her babies."

"I thought as much."

She saw a small cart on the other side of the door and walked to it, hoping he'd disappear again. The cart was rusty and impossible to pull. Maybe some oil on those wheels?

"What are you doing?"

Sarah stared at him. He was a few inches taller than Ron Broadwell, but Ron was stockier. It was hard to tell what size Jack was under those horrible, old clothes.

Not that she was wondering what he looked like under his clothes. She didn't think of him that way. Her face was just hot from the sun shining on it. *Really?* She was too old to get embarrassed thinking about any man. And why was she comparing Ron to Jack? She needed to get back to her old life—maybe improve on her old life.

"I'm looking for a wagon or something to pull some pumpkins to the car. I want to give some to Mr. Pope for cutting the grass."

"He doesn't need anything for cutting the grass."

"Maybe you don't think so. But I'm going to the barn-raising tomorrow, and I want to take something with me."

"You surprise me. I don't surprise easy." He slowly smiled at her.

"Thanks, I guess." She walked away from the rusted cart. "It doesn't matter. I'll just pick a few and put them in the car."

"I have a better idea. Wait right here."

He went into the barn. Sarah didn't know what to expect, but she waited. Maybe he was going to offer to help her move the pumpkins. Or maybe he decided to take a nap. What did he do all day every day out here?

She heard the sound of an engine starting inside the barn. There were double doors on the other side. She ran to see what was going on.

Jack came out on an old tractor, pulling a large cart behind it. She remembered her grandfather driving that tractor. She didn't remember it being so loud.

"I didn't know it still worked," she shouted above the sound.

"Of course it still works."

"Why didn't you cut the grass then?" she asked. "Wouldn't that have been easier?"

"You can't use a cart to cut grass," he yelled back. "This is the only equipment that's left. I'll meet you in the pumpkin patch."

Sarah stood aside as he went by. The awful smell of diesel made her put her hand over her nose. She didn't remember that part either. She took a quick glance inside the barn at Jack's living quarters. It looked like the same old blanket on a bale of straw that she'd seen sixteen years ago.

He drove the tractor and cart down the wide path between the areas where the pumpkins grew. Some of the vines were in the way, but he rolled over them. Most were trained off the path to allow easy access to the pumpkins.

The biggest ones were at the top of the hill where they received plenty of sunlight and shade from a few large trees. Jack stopped the tractor there and got down. Sarah sighed as she looked over the large pumpkins that were dark orange in the sun.

"Here." He handed her a wide knife and a pair of gloves. "You cut the ones you want. I'll put them in the cart."

"Really?" It was hard for her to believe that he actually

meant to help.

"Sure. How else would we do it? I didn't think you'd been gone that long."

Sarah started to explain what she'd meant but gave up and headed toward the biggest pumpkin she saw. She had to keep from running to it as she had when she was a child. It was still exciting seeing that first enormous pumpkin and knowing it was for her.

Who knew it would still be that way?

Jack was as good as his word. She used the knife to cut the thick vine that held each pumpkin in place. He picked it up and took it to the cart. It wasn't long until they had a big stack of them in the back.

She smiled when she saw them heaped up. "That's a lot of pumpkins."

"Yes it is. Is that how many you want to take?"

"Probably. I don't want to overwhelm them with pumpkins." She forgot who she was talking to for a moment and grinned in the joy of the moment. Her face was hot and sweaty, and her tennis shoes were full of mud. But she'd had a good time.

"You had that front tooth fixed, didn't you?" he observed.

How could he have noticed so much about her and she barely remembered him—except for that stupid kiss?

"I actually lost that tooth that was chipped," she said. "It was still a baby tooth."

She looked at his face—or tried to. It was difficult to see around the thick beard. She wondered what he really looked like under there.

"Looking for my baby teeth?" he asked.

"Sorry." She shook her head. "I wasn't looking at your teeth." Sarah gave up trying to figure out what he really looked like. Why did she care?

"What then?"

"I don't know. Just wondering what you looked like without the beard, I guess. I can't remember what you looked like when I saw you last."

He didn't say anything, just got on the tractor and pulled the wagon out of the pumpkin patch.

Sarah felt like an idiot and hoped she hadn't given him the wrong idea. He wasn't exactly the kind of man she was used to being around. She took off her gloves and followed the tractor back to the barn.

He stopped and looked down at her. "I'll take these over to Gray."

"Okay. Thanks."

"Well?"

"What?"

"Aren't you coming?"

"I, uh…"

"You can ride up here with me," he offered. "There's plenty of room."

"No. That's okay. I'll ride back here with the pumpkins." She smiled up at him.

"Suit yourself."

She climbed up over the pumpkins. Their skins were thick—she didn't have to worry about damaging them. Finally she found a perch and settled back for the ride after signaling Jack that she was ready.

Sarah remembered doing this plenty of times as a kid. Sometimes Kathy was with her. They'd take the pumpkins down to the stand by the road where they sold them to people who couldn't make the trek out to the patch.

The field was bumpy as they passed through it. It was difficult to maintain her seat, but she finally balanced herself holding on to the wood sides of the wagon. She was going to feel the strain of that, and walking around the rough pumpkin patch, tomorrow. It was a lot more work than she was used to.

"How's it going back there?" Jack called out as they crested the hill before the land dropped down toward Mr. Pope's farm.

"I'm fine," she called out and waved.

"Hold on tight," he said as the tractor climbed up and over the rise.

Sarah held on, gritting her teeth. She didn't plan to fall out of the wagon and have to see his smirk because she didn't ride up front with him. Pumpkins weren't the most comfortable things to sit on. They kept shifting. She lost her balance several times and had to climb up on top again, but she didn't fall off the wagon.

Once the land leveled out, she was steadier but glad she didn't have to ride back with the pumpkins they'd cut. How had she ever thought this was fun?

Jack took the tractor between the large, two-story house and the site where all the building materials were. She guessed that's where the new barn was going up.

Mr. Pope was working on an outside pump that gushed water. He stopped when he saw them and walked over. "What's all this?"

"Sarah wanted to give you some pumpkins," Jack explained as he shut off the tractor engine.

"That's nice of you." Mr. Pope smiled at Sarah who was still in the wagon. "Need some help getting out of there?"

"No. I'm fine." She laughed like she wasn't worried about the pumpkins shifting as she tried to climb out. "I just wanted to say thanks for cutting the grass."

"You're welcome. I hope you're coming to the barn-raising tomorrow," he said.

"I am. Should I bring anything?"

Mr. Pope glanced at the pumpkins. "I think you've brought enough. Thanks."

"What's going on over there with the pump?" Jack asked.

"Darn thing broke on me this morning. I think it's the seal."

"Let me take a look."

Sarah took that opportunity to climb out of the wagon in case she fell on her face. The pumpkins kept shifting as she moved her weight toward the back. She held on to the sides, but it didn't help her moving across the round, slippery edges of the pumpkins.

As they were looking at the pump, she managed to reach the back where all she had to do was move one leg across one of the big pumpkins and she'd be home free. Unfortunately, her leg refused to move from under her, where it had become trapped between two other pumpkins. As she attempted that last drop out of the wagon, she fell forward and was trapped half off the back of it.

"Looks like you could use a hand." Jack's voice was edged with humor as he stood over her.

She could only see his boots which had seen better days a dozen or so years before. "I can get it. Go fix the pump."

"It's fixed. Let me help you."

"I'm fine. Just go away."

"You're very stubborn."

Before she could reply, he put his hands at her waist and lifted her off the back of the wagon.

"Thanks. But I was okay."

"You're welcome. You didn't look like it."

Mrs. Pope and one of the couple's grandsons came out to help get the pumpkins off the wagon. They made a huge pile near the tables that had been set up for the food that would be laid out for the barn-raising.

"That's a lot of pumpkins." Twelve-year-old David Pope admired them. "Can I have one?"

"Sure," Sarah said. "Or you're welcome to come pick your own before Monday."

David looked at his grandparents. "Can we do that?"

"We can." Mary Pope introduced herself to Sarah. "You two stay for supper. I've got some cornbread in the oven and some pinto beans on the stove. You can get washed up in the house."

Sarah thought Jack might say he couldn't stay. She didn't want to put the Popes out if she lost her ride home, so she waited to see what he was going to do.

"Thanks," he finally said. "Sounds good."

They were turning to go into the house when Sheriff Morgan pulled up. Everyone waited until he got out.

"Afternoon." He nodded. "Gray. Mary. Ms. Tucker. I've got a few questions I need to ask Jack, if you don't mind. I don't want to get in the middle of something."

"Not in the middle of anything, Bill," Mr. Pope said. "We're about to have supper. Ask your questions and then stay to eat."

Chapter Ten

Mary asked for her help inside. Sarah offered to take glasses of iced tea out to Jack and the sheriff as they sat on the wide porch talking. Grayson Pope had gone upstairs to wash, dragging his grandson with him as he went.

"I know you've had people out there trying to dig up that gold." Sarah heard Sheriff Morgan as she came to the screen door. She waited to hear Jack's quiet reply.

"You know I have. Where's the question?"

"George Burris was looking for it too. We found some pictures of you throwing him off the property. Not the night he was killed but sometime during the spring from the look of it."

"Still waiting for the question, Bill."

"I'm not accusing you of killing George, mind you. But I'd like to know who else you've caught out there looking for the gold. I started thinking about who might want to kill George—and how it relates to all that info he wanted to give

Ms. Tucker."

Sheriff Morgan sounded relaxed, not worried about anything Jack might take away with the questioning. Jack seemed a little on edge to her. Was he worried that the sheriff was getting too close to the truth?

"I suppose that makes sense."

"Any names you can think of? I know you tied up that Bradley boy when he was out there with a pick and shovel. But he's away at college now, so he's not a suspect."

"Just a minute." Jack glanced back. "Something you wanted, Sarah?"

She pushed open the screen door and handed them each a glass of tea. "Sorry. Just wondering what was going on."

"No reason you shouldn't hear too," Sheriff Morgan said. "Jack has thrown a few treasure hunters off your property down through the years. Just wondering if any of them come to mind as more serious than others."

"Thanks, Sarah." Jack sipped his tea. "I can't think of anyone I couldn't persuade to look elsewhere for gold. There weren't any returns. Sorry."

"I get it." The sheriff nodded. "I picked Bradley up that day. He'd wet himself. I had one of the treasure hunters you sent on their way come back to have me arrest you for roughing him up. Since he was trespassing in the first place, I showed him the door."

"I can't believe people are serious about Confederate gold," Sarah added. "It seems like a fable to me."

"When that fable involves gold bullion, people get real serious about it," Jack assured her.

"It's real," the sheriff said. "The folks at the historical society say so. You should have a word with them about it. You'd be surprised what you can find buried out here."

Sarah wasn't looking forward to finding treasure or anything else. "I barely remember my grandparents talking about it when I was a kid."

"They loved you," Jack said. "They didn't want to fill your head with that kind of rubbish."

"Well if anything comes to mind," the sheriff said, "let me know. I'm out of ideas as to why anyone would want to kill old George. I'm going to his funeral tomorrow and hoping the killer might turn up. It happens sometimes."

"I'll let you know if I think of anyone," Jack agreed.

They went in the house and sat around the old wood table. There was cornbread and beans, plus fried squash and fresh tomatoes. Mary pulled out a large peach pie she'd baked from the last of the summer peaches. The iced tea was plentiful and the conversation ranged from what crops were bringing the best price to residents of Misty River threatening to create a town to keep their land from being gobbled up by other cities.

Most of the issues were things Sarah couldn't talk about because she didn't know enough about them to have an opinion. She knew Clare had been approached by several small communities in her district that wanted to become towns. Many were being annexed by Richmond, Suffolk, and the bigger cities. It was only a matter of time before the areas started growing as bedroom communities. Sometimes residents weren't happy with that designation.

Sarah didn't mention that she worked for Clare. She didn't want the pleasant dinner to end with the Popes or the sheriff asking her to talk to her boss about various subjects that she could influence. She'd been in similar situations that had turned into arguments.

She didn't expect that from these people, but she didn't want to risk it. The conversation eventually turned to plans for her grandparents' property over coffee.

"I have a buyer who wants the land for the river access," she admitted.

Mary and Gray exchanged glances over the table.

"That's gotta be Leland Drake," Gray said. "He's all hopped up about this Blue Way thing on the river. He's got the only other piece of riverfront in Misty River. Everything else is owned by the state."

"Yes. He told me," Sarah said. "I was just glad he didn't

want to build apartments or something. I'd hate to see the land chopped up that way."

"You wouldn't sell to someone like that, would you?" David asked. "That would be terrible. No more pumpkins."

The adults at the table shifted uneasily in their chairs.

"Sarah doesn't live here," Mary explained. "She has to sell the land to someone. It would be better to keep the property in one piece, even if tourists would be going in and out with their kayaks."

Sarah felt bad about David's question. He didn't understand the circumstances, but didn't she feel the same about wanting a family to live there again instead of a commercial enterprise? Maybe she didn't understand either.

"At least it will keep Jack from taking out those treasure hunters!" Gray laughed.

"That's true," Sheriff Morgan agreed. "Maybe Leland will hire you to be security on the property for his Blue Way."

There was no answering smile from Jack. The conversation changed quickly before Sheriff Morgan said his goodbyes.

Jack and Sarah left a few minutes later. It was still only about seven-thirty, but everyone was going to be up at dawn for the barn-raising. It was a night they all needed to turn in early.

She still refused to ride on the tractor with Jack. She sat in the wagon again. It was easier to hang on, but she was sure her backside was going to be bruised when it was over. Without the pumpkins, there was nothing but a hard slab of wood between her and the bumps in the field.

The blue sky was turning pale pink and purple and there was a sliver of a crescent moon coming up on the horizon. She looked at it thoughtfully, not used to spending time between work and home gazing at the star-filled sky. It was beautiful.

"Almost there," Jack said. "How are you holding up?"

"Okay," she yelled back. She was going to be glad to get

out of the wagon. Without the pumpkins in the way, she wouldn't have a problem this time.

Eating dinner with the Pope family reminded her so much of spending time with her grandparents. David was lucky to have them. She tried not to feel that her time with her grandmother and grandfather had been cut too short. Even if they hadn't disappeared, her mother had been intent on taking the new job in Richmond. Sarah's visits with them would probably have been more limited.

But what glorious times those would have been.

Jack drove the tractor beside the barn and turned off the engine. "Looks like you've got company."

She glanced toward the drive and saw a dark Lincoln Town Car. It was her mother.

"Thanks for helping me with the pumpkins." Sarah turned back to him. "I think I got a little too ambitious on how many I was taking. It just seems like such a waste for them to die on the vine."

"They don't die. They keep growing. I suppose the new owner will bulldoze the whole pumpkin patch."

They both looked at the mist swirling through the pumpkins, highlighted by the moon.

"What will you do, Jack?"

"What I always do—survive. Goodnight, Sarah."

"Goodnight."

She didn't look back at his solitary figure as she walked to the house. She couldn't make decisions about selling the property because the pumpkin patch would be gone and a man she barely knew would be out of a home. Her mother would put her back on track about selling the farm. There would be no question in her mind what to do.

Her mother was waiting on the back porch, a glass in her hand and a bottle of champagne next to her. Sandra Denning Tucker was well-dressed in a tan designer suit with matching pumps. Her hair was almost the same blond shade as Sarah's. She was thinner, though, and after several uses of Botox, she actually had fewer wrinkles, even though she was almost thirty years older.

"It's about time. Where have you been?"

Sarah sat beside her. She didn't know how long her mother had been there, but this wasn't her first bottle of champagne. "I was at the Popes eating dinner. I didn't remember how nice they were—I'm not sure I remember them at all. Their grandson was there."

"That's very friendly of you. Are you thinking of staying?"

"No, of course not. Why are you here? I'm sure whatever you have to say could've been on the phone or text."

Sandra lifted her glass to the property before them. "I thought I'd have one last look. I grew up here, you know."

"And hated every minute of it. Yes, I know. I hope you have a driver." Sarah knew from her mother's slurred words that she'd had too much to drink.

"Of course, dear. I brought Charlie with me. At least I think his name is Charlie. It's something like that." Her mother brought out another glass and poured champagne with an unsteady hand. She gave it to Sarah.

"What are we celebrating?"

"Getting rid of this albatross that's been hanging around my neck for the last sixteen years. And for a nice profit too, I might mention. Thanks to you. Dusty is hopeless at this kind of thing. I swear sometimes that boy is going to end up in the Peace Corps or something. He has no head for business."

Sarah carefully sipped from the overfilled glass. "Thanks for the champagne and for coming out to tell me about Dusty. Now, why are you really here?"

Jack started up the tractor, and Sandra jumped, clinging to her daughter's arm. "What in the world is that?"

"The tractor. I imagine Jack is taking it back in the barn."

"You've been using a tractor? What were you doing with it?"

"Taking pumpkins to the Popes for their barn-raising

tomorrow."

Close up now, her mother stared at her as though she were a stranger. "What are you doing out here, Sarah? And who is Jack? Don't tell me you've become infatuated with some local farm boy. Nothing good can come of it. I know from experience."

Sarah let that information go, but she was curious. She'd never heard about her mother's farm boy romance.

"Jack has been here since Grandma and Grandpa lived here. They took him in for a while to get him away from his abusive father. Now he lives out here and takes care of the place."

Sandra sat up straight and squared her shoulders. "You've gone off the deep end. Maybe you should go home and I'll take care of the rest of the problem."

"I'm not infatuated with Jack—or anyone else. My divorce was only recently final, remember? I'm not in any frame of mind to think about anyone romantically. You don't have to worry about me. I know why I'm here, and I'm not Dusty. I'll take care of it."

Her mother sighed and sipped more champagne before she leaned her head against Sarah's shoulder. "Yes. You are my levelheaded, ambitious daughter. Thank you."

"So why are you here?" Sarah repeated.

"There's another snag in selling the land. I'm sorry. I can't find the deed. It doesn't mean there isn't one. It just means that you'll have to get a copy from the courthouse."

"At least that makes sense. Don't worry. I'll get a copy of the deed. I should have everything wrapped up Monday and be able to head home."

"You're such a good girl." Sandra's words were fading as her head slipped lower on Sarah's shoulder.

"Don't pass out on me. I can't move you. Get up, Mom. Let's get you out to the car. Come on."

But it was too late. Her mother had passed out, her head slipping to Sarah's lap. She was gently snoring in the next few seconds.

"Thanks, Mom." Sarah sighed. She'd have to get out from under her and get Charlie to put her in the car. "I'm sure glad we had this visit."

"Problems?" Jack asked though she couldn't see him in the shadows.

"This is my mother, Sandra."

"We've met. Want me to take her upstairs?"

"No. I'd hate to think how that would end. Her head might explode in the morning. Her driver is in the car. I just have to get her out there."

"Allow me."

He stepped in front of her and gently put his hands under Sandra's back and legs, lifting her like a child.

"Thanks. I'll run ahead and alert her driver."

But when Sarah reached the car two steps ahead of Jack, Charlie was snoring, his head thrown back, mouth open, in the driver's seat. She couldn't wake him when she called his name and shook him.

"Smells like he's had a few too many. I think your mother needs a new driver," Jack observed. "Upstairs then?"

"Sorry. Yes. Thanks. We'll leave him here. He can sleep it off in the car."

Sarah tried to get ahead of him and turn on the lights but Jack was in the house before her. Nimble-footed and knowing the way, he reached her grandparent's old bedroom in the dark without her help. He lay Sandra gently on the bed and backed away.

"I hope her head doesn't explode in the morning," Jack said. "Why does she hate this place so much?"

"I don't think she hates it. I think she's just afraid she might have to live here again." Sarah removed her mother's shoes and pulled the quilt over her.

She and Jack went downstairs together.

"Guess that means you're spending the night?"

"I guess so." She put her hands in her pockets and looked up at him. "I'm sorry you're going to lose your home. I know you don't want me to say that, but I wish it could be different.”

“It’s your life. It can be however you want it to be.”

She watched him walk out the door before she went upstairs to her mother’s old room and fell asleep in her clothes.

Chapter Eleven

It was still dark when Sarah felt a hand at her shoulder and heard a voice telling her it was time to wake up.

In that instant, she realized that she'd forgotten to set the alarm on her phone.

"It's five-thirty," Jack said. "You don't want to be late. Mary makes a great breakfast."

She rolled over with a groan. "Really? You eat breakfast at this time of day?"

"I think most people do. Do you want me to wake your mother?"

"No!" She sat up, completely awake at the suggestion. "Don't do that. Let's hope she wakes up while I'm gone."

"Okay. Your call."

Sarah was going to thank him for waking her, but he was gone.

It was going to be another day scrounging for clothes. At least she had the tennis shoes, even though she had to scrape mud off them. She switched on the overhead light and started searching for another pair of jeans and a top.

Thirty minutes later, she was ready to go. She'd looked in on her mother, who hadn't moved all night. She wrote her a brief note and left it on the bedside table. It included a line about hiring a new driver.

It was still too early for breakfast, but she wanted to participate in the barn-raising and had promised to meet Ron there. She'd heard the tractor start up before she was ready and guessed that Jack had already left. Luckily, her mother's car wasn't parked behind hers. She got in her rental car and crept out of the driveway.

She hadn't been joking when she told Jack that she didn't want to be around when her mother woke up and discovered she'd spent the night in her parent's old home. There was bound to be fireworks and recriminations. Since her mother's visit had also come with news that there were other legal documents that weren't ready for the sale, Sarah felt like she had enough on her plate.

Her mother's actions still puzzled her. It wasn't like Sandra to get drunk. She wasn't against having a few drinks, but overindulging in anything wasn't her style.

Did she regret the sale of her home but didn't feel like she could say anything about it? That would make sense of the champagne and coming here to tell Sarah about the deed. Maybe there was still some part of her childhood that she didn't want to let go.

Dusty would laugh at that. Their mother loved living in the city and stayed away from anyplace that didn't have paved roads and coffee shops.

The intersection was empty as Sarah turned to go to the Pope's house. Apparently not everyone in Misty River was up at five-thirty. But there were enough people out and about that there were dozens of cars and pickups at Mary and Gray's house. The sky was getting lighter, banishing the shadows to beyond the trees.

"There you are!" Kathy found her right after Sarah had

parked her car. "You overslept, didn't you? City folk. I can't believe you can sleep past six a.m."

"How long have you been here?"

"I've been here since four helping Mary get breakfast ready. It's the most important meal of the day, you know. Especially when you've got a bunch of men ready to help put up your barn. I don't think I've ever made that much grits."

"I hope you made some protein bars too," Sarah said. "That's all I usually eat until dinner."

"Protein bars?" Kathy hugged her. "Just eat some sausages and pretend they're protein sticks. You'll be fine."

"I hope there's coffee."

"You know it. You gotta have coffee for all those hungry men too."

They walked up to the house together. The tables out front were loaded with eggs, bacon, sausage, pancakes, and grits. Some of the men were already eating, sitting on the grass or steps. A few tree stumps made good tables.

Even Sarah had to admit that everything smelled delicious. She couldn't remember when she'd eaten food like this in the morning—or at any other time for that matter.

Ron found them as Kathy kept putting food on Sarah's plate. "Morning, ladies. Nothing like a good breakfast before the hard work kicks in."

"Good morning," Sarah said. "Kathy, I'm not eating grits. I didn't like it as a kid. I don't want it now."

"But I stirred it. That has to mean something."

"Does it have cheese in it?" Ron asked. "I only like it with cheese."

"You two are just not any fun. Eat what you want. I can eat enough grits for the three of us." She popped a big biscuit on Sarah's plate. "You have to try these too."

Sarah waited with her heaping plate in her hands as Ron filled a plate for himself. She didn't recognize most of the people around them at the table, and the chances were that she looked too different to be recognizable.

"Coffee?" a voice said from behind her.

She recognized Jack's voice—it was very distinctive—and the first thing she'd heard that morning. She turned and reached for the coffee he was offering and then stopped to stare.

"Jack?"

"Coffee." He put the large cup in her hand when she didn't take it from him.

"Is that really you?" Sarah had wondered what he really looked like since she'd met him again. To suddenly see him with no beard and dressed in decent jeans and a T-shirt was amazing.

"You said you wanted to know what I look like under the beard. Here I am."

She couldn't stop staring. He was actually very good-looking. Without the huge beard, he had high cheekbones and a lean face. His dark eyebrows and thick lashes framed his intensely blue eyes. He'd cut his hair short too.

"You know, it's not nice to stare."

"Sorry." She managed to smile at him. "I'm just—surprised."

"Jack?" Ron said with a laugh. "I wouldn't have recognized you, man. Was it time for the spring thaw or something? I've never seen you without the beard."

"You're handsome!" Kathy exclaimed. "Don't stand around here talking to them. I have some ladies who are dying to meet you."

Sarah started to say something to keep him from leaving, but no words came out. She had a dozen questions she wanted to ask. Maybe it was for the best that Kathy took him away. It already felt like he was too entwined in her life.

Jack shrugged as Kathy put her arm through his and led him away. Sarah smiled at Ron and made small talk as they ate. She thought there was a good chance that her friend might be interested in Jack. The way she'd talked about the man she liked made it sound as though it could be someone she worked with. Maybe she had wanted to be with Jack even when he'd looked like a mountain man.

As soon as breakfast was over, everyone was put to work doing something. Roosters were crowing as the sun began to move through the trees that separated the Pope farm from Sarah's. Saws began buzzing, and hammers were loud as nails were tapped into wood that would create the frame for the barn.

Sarah didn't have any skills that related to barn-building. Mary gave her easy things to do such as making sure everyone was hydrated and being an errand girl if someone ran out of nails or other small items.

Kathy was actually helping with the frame, laughing with Ron and Jack as well as a tall man in a brown Stetson. Sarah made sure the water bucket was passed around but kept her eyes on them, envious of her friend's ease around the men and tools.

Most of her time was taken staring at Jack as he worked. She hated to think that she was so shallow that he'd turn her head now that he was cleaned up. But he had looked really bad, in all fairness. And he was a squatter—even though he was a protective squatter with a purpose.

It wasn't like she wanted to date him or anything, she argued with herself as she kept looking around for him while she passed out water. She was just really surprised that he cleaned up so well. And maybe this would be good for him. Maybe someone would see him this way and hire him to do something besides hang around a farm that was about to be sold out from under him.

Her phone rang in her pocket. It was her mother. She was embarrassed and angry about passing out on the porch last night.

"You didn't have to prod me to look for a new driver," Sandra said. "As soon as we get back to Richmond, he's out. Where are you?"

"At the barn-raising next door."

"Why? You don't know anything about building. You're letting your emotions run away with you on this. I understand. It happened to me too when I got here last night.

That's why it's such a good thing that the land will belong to someone else on Monday. We have to put this behind us. Neither one of us is cut out to live on a farm."

"I don't know anything about building. You're right. I'm just helping out because Mr. Pope has been kind to me. It's not going to stop me from selling the farm. I know where I belong. I'll see you when I get home Monday—or if there's anything else you've forgotten to tell me about the property."

"You have a right to be angry with me." Sandra's voice faltered. "I screwed this up. I guess I didn't want to admit that Mom and Dad were really gone. I know that it's been a long time. I-I should've accepted it by now. It's just hard sometimes not knowing what happened to them. I wish we'd found out before we sold the land. It feels like giving up."

Sarah couldn't believe her mother admitted to feeling similar to her. "We don't have to give up. Even if we sell the land, we can hire people to look for them."

"I did that at the beginning."

"I know. But that was then. Let's do it again, but hire more private detectives. This is the information age. Someone knows where they went, Mom. Let's keep going until we know too."

Sandra sniffled. "You're right. I felt silly at the time. Your father kept saying they just didn't want us to know where they'd gone. I knew that was wrong, but I tried to ignore the way I felt about it. If you'll help me, maybe this time will be different. We'll talk about it when you get back. I love you. Be careful. I was looking at the living room where that man was killed. Are you sure Jack doesn't have something to do with it?"

"I am," Sarah said confidently. "And the sheriff is too. I have to go. I love you. I'll see you at home."

Mary was looking for her. She waved as soon as Sarah looked up from her phone call. "Let's get some water over there to Tom and Rick. They're the ones putting the sides of the barn together. I'm worried about Rick. He's just over the flu. His wife called to make sure he had plenty to drink."

"Sure. Sorry. That was my mother."

"Sandra? She's out here too? Why didn't she come with you? We haven't seen her in a long time."

"She's headed back to Richmond," Sarah said. "Let me get more water for Rick and Tom."

There were more than two men working on the barn wall nailing long pieces of wood to two-by-fours. Sarah gave them all water and ran out. She had to go back to the pump in the front yard to refill the bucket.

She looked up to see Kathy on one of the high rafters, flirting and hammering nails beside Jack. He seemed to be flirting too, a grin on his face as he talked with her.

As if he felt her watching him, Jack turned his head and waved. Sarah pretended not to see him. She filled up the bucket and headed toward one of the other crews who were working on the barn's foundation.

As the day progressed toward noon, the barn was taking shape. Mary asked for her help with lunch. Luckily it was small things because Sarah wasn't much of a cook either. There were several women helping in the kitchen. She did her part and tried not to feel inadequate. She was just out of her element, as her mother had said. She never felt this way back home.

The women took the huge portions of ham, green beans, potatoes and cornbread to the tables. Mary rang a bell on the porch for lunch. There was plenty of fried chicken and biscuits, peach cobblers, banana pudding, and homemade ice cream with gallons of sweet tea to wash everything down.

Ron had stopped working when he had a call from the sheriff's department. He paused to let Sarah know that he was leaving. "Sorry I can't stay for lunch, but this is the way my life is. I'll try to come back if I can."

"Sure," she said as she put out a bowl of jellied cranberries.

"Maybe I shouldn't ask right away, but I know you're leaving soon. What about lunch or supper tomorrow?"

Sarah considered it. Sunday loomed long and empty as

she waited for Monday morning to get everything else done. "I'd like that. Thanks for asking."

"Great." He smiled and kissed her cheek. "I'll call you when I know what time I'll be free."

"Maybe I should give you my cell phone number."

"Yeah." He laughed. "I was just going to look it up on the sheriff's report, but that would be better. And this is mine."

They exchanged numbers, and Ron waved as he went to his car.

"He's leaving already," Jack said. "Was it the work or the date?"

"Not exactly a date," she corrected, feeling self-conscious with him now. Before, she only felt threatened and annoyed. "You should probably wash up for lunch. Mary says there's lots of work to do this afternoon."

"But tomorrow is the *real* date?"

"You're an eavesdropper," Sarah told him.

"That's how I know everything. I'll be back."

She determined that she would be busy ladling out food or pouring tea when she saw him again. Her mother was right about one thing—she couldn't let herself feel bad for Jack. He needed to move on and get a life of his own. The more she spent time with him and people who praised him for taking care of the farm, the guiltier she felt making him leave what little he had.

Kathy was with the tall man in the Stetson. She seemed to be flirting with him too. Sarah wasn't sure if Jack was the man whose butt Kathy was admiring or if it was this man.

"Hey, I want you to meet Ben Reece. He's my manager. The farm has run better than ever since he signed on. Ben, this is Sarah Tucker. She owns the property next door."

Ben was very sincere as he shook hands with Sarah. "Nice to meet you, ma'am."

While he was talking to her, Kathy was behind him making faces and pointing to his rear end. Sarah smiled despite herself. Obviously this was Mr. Right. She was relieved that her friend wasn't interested in Jack—she told herself it was because he was leaving and Kathy might not see him again.

"I offered Jack a job this morning," Ben said. "He's a hard worker, and he's taken good care of your place with no supervision. I think we could use a man like him."

"That would be wonderful," Sarah replied. "I hope he took you up on it."

"He said he'd think about it," Kathy told her. "I'm going to fill up a plate and sit over there in the shade. How 'bout you, Ben?"

"Sounds good to me." He glanced at Sarah. "You'd be welcome to join us."

Kathy was shaking her head and sticking out her tongue.

"I have a few other things I have to do before I eat," Sarah lied. Kathy was very clear on wanting to be alone with him. "But thanks for asking."

When Ben went to get some corn on the cob, Kathy nudged her with her elbow. "He better not be interested in you."

"It doesn't matter," Sarah reminded her. "I'm leaving Monday, remember?"

"You should take Jack with you. But don't you look at Ben again with those baby blue eyes."

Sarah laughed as she watched her friend walk off with him. She couldn't believe Kathy couldn't get things going with the handsome cowboy when he was there every day working for her.

Almost everyone had already grabbed a plate and found a place to sit. Sarah had noticed some shade on the other side of the house, so she took her plate and a glass of tea over there and sat in the pleasant garden area.

"Is this seat taken?" Jack asked.

"I don't think so." She sat up a little straighter and almost spilled her tea. "I should warn you before you sit down that I know nothing about barn building or farming. My conversation is limited to political things happening in the state and possibly a few things about social media."

"I'll take my chances." He sat beside her. "Nice spot."

"That's what I thought."

"Sorry Ron had to leave. I could tell by the way he kept looking for you while we were working that he thinks a lot of you."

"We only met when George died. Most of the time he's been taking my statements about dead men and asking what I was doing while they were being killed. I'm not sure that's enough to have a relationship."

"I don't know. I've known couples who had less in common." He took a sip of tea. "But you're leaving anyway. Not many long distance relationships work out."

She laughed. "I don't think I'd call living in Richmond a long distance relationship with someone who lives in Misty River."

"I suppose that's true."

They both were quiet as they ate. A crow called from the nearby pear tree, and bees buzzed as they collected pollen from the flowers in the garden.

"Thanks again for helping me with my mother," she said. "I thought she'd be okay, but I didn't know about her driver."

"That's okay. How is she this morning?"

Sarah stared at the tall flowers to keep from looking into his eyes as she spoke. "I think she's sad about selling the farm—not sad enough to want to live here again. She hates the country now. But it was her home at one time."

"That's why she was drinking?"

"I think so. It's not really like her. I don't know. We both wish there had been an answer to what happened to my grandparents." She looked back at him. "Do you have any ideas?"

"No. I'm sorry. I wish I did. They were very good to me. I'd repay that kindness if I could."

"I'd say you've done that, looking after the place for so long."

"That was nothing. I needed a place to stay when I got out of the army. Tommy and Bess were gone. None of their family seemed as interested in their land as the treasure hunters."

"Do you believe the gold is real?"

"They do," he replied. "And they'll keep coming as long as the legend continues."

Chapter Twelve

After lunch, Jack went back to work on the roof with Kathy and Ben. Sarah watched the three of them nailing down large sheets of plywood after it was lifted with a pulley system.

Two sides of the barn went up. Mary and Sarah started painting as soon as a wall was secure.

"You know Gray wanted to paint it blue or orange. Can you imagine?" Mary asked her. "I told him a barn is supposed to be red."

Sarah had been lost in her thoughts about her property and didn't respond right away. "Oh. Sorry. Yes. I know what you mean. I guess a barn wouldn't have to be red, but it follows tradition to paint it red."

Mary put down her paint brush. "Honey, you seem troubled about something."

"Just worried about treasure hunters, I guess." Sarah smiled.

"Treasure hunters have been coming out there since before your mother was born. Tommy handled them. You will too."

"I think it would help if they thought the treasure had been found."

"I suppose it would, but people have been digging holes out here for a long time and haven't found a thing. It's just a story."

Sarah agreed and went back to painting. She was grateful to Mary for trying to help her see another angle. But the truth was that she couldn't wait past Monday after she'd settled all the paperwork. She had to go home and get back to work.

After that, the gold, the land, and the Blue Way would be in Leland's capable hands. He'd have to deal with the problem.

The barn was mostly up before dinner. There were still shingles that needed to go on the roof and painting that had to be done. The workers stopped again to eat around six p.m. The food was a mixture of leftovers from lunch and big hunks of homemade bread and potato salad to go with them. Many of the men made huge sandwiches with the ham and chicken.

Sarah looked for Jack. He was helping Gray and Ben put up the doors on the front of the barn. Mary kept calling for them to stop and eat. Gray said he'd be there when he was done.

"I guess you've stayed about as long as you can." Kathy nibbled on a piece of fried chicken. She kept her eyes on Ben as he worked. "I'm going to be sorry to see you go."

Sarah had no appetite, despite spending the day outside working. "It's been nice connecting with you again. But you're right. After I get a copy of the deed for Mace and make sure the paperwork is good on the legal aspect of my grandparents being gone, I have to go home."

"You're sure about this, right?" Kathy's eyes narrowed on hers. "You have to sell the property?"

"Yes. We can't just leave it like this anymore. I don't expect Jack to keep taking care of it. It would fall apart. It's best to sell it."

"What about a trust? You could put it in a trust for a future generation that might want to live here and raise pumpkins."

"That's an idea," Sarah agreed. "I suppose Jack could keep an eye on it since he'll be working for you."

"I wish he was. But he turned Ben down. I don't know where he's going from here or what he'll do. But he doesn't want to work for me."

Sarah considered why Jack wouldn't want the opportunity to live close to where he'd been for the past sixteen years. It was probably the best offer he'd get. She decided to talk to him about it when she saw him later.

As they were finishing their meal, Jack and Ben joined them with heaping plates of food.

"You two eat like birds," Ben said. "Especially you, Sarah. You need to eat some bread. Put some meat on those bones."

Her face felt hot, but she smiled at him. "I don't work this hard often enough to eat like that. Mostly attorneys sit behind a computer."

"Besides that," Kathy observed, "she's got some good-looking bones, right, Jack?"

He was saved from responding when someone picked up a fiddle and started playing with another man on the banjo. The music was simple and fast. It didn't take long before a few older couples started dancing.

"Want to dance, Ben?" Kathy said it like it didn't mean a thing to her one way or another.

"Sure. Why not?"

She stood up and grabbed his hand with a wink at Sarah.

"I think she likes him," Jack observed.

"That's Kathy," Sarah agreed. "I'm going to head home. I don't know where they get the energy to dance after working all day."

Jack got to his feet. “You have to stay for at least one dance. It’s part of putting up the barn.” He held out his hand to her.

She glanced at the happy faces of the dancers as they cheered and whirled around the yard. “I don’t dance. Not like that anyway. Thanks.”

“Like what? All you have to do is move your feet and smile. You can do it.”

“Jack—”

“Sarah.” He smiled, grabbed her hand, and pulled her slowly up beside him. “You can do this.”

“All right,” she finally agreed. She’d dance once with him and then go back to the hotel. What could it hurt?

The front yard had been mostly trampled down by the delivery of supplies for the barn and then by people working. It made a good dance floor. A few younger couples were dancing to the lively music but most of the older people had moved to the porch. The younger couples cut loose with all kinds of crazy moves that had nothing to do with country dancing and everything to do with creativity.

Kathy and Ben were one of those couples. Even David was dancing with a teenage girl.

Sarah panicked when she and Jack actually got in the middle of the wild dancing. “Really, I appreciate it, but I don’t think I can do this.”

As soon as the words were out of her mouth, the tempo of the music changed to a slow dance. Kathy quickly pushed herself against Ben’s chest, and his arms went around her. David hurriedly left the dance area followed by the girl who tried to call him back.

Some of the older couples returned to sway slowly to the music under the silver crescent moon that was hanging in the sky above them.

“How about this?” Jack asked before she could leave the dance area.

Feeling a little trapped, Sarah nodded, putting one hand in his and the other on his shoulder. She knew how to waltz.

Most of the people around them were kind of standing in one place and swaying back and forth. She could do this, and then she'd go to the hotel.

Jack didn't press her to get closer. She was grateful for that. Even so, she felt awkward and uneasy. There was no explanation for it. When she traveled with Clare, she was required to handle dozens of social situations that came up. Normally that wasn't a problem for her. This was different somehow. She didn't want to think about why.

"You're a very good dancer," he said in a muted tone. "I don't know why you got so shy."

"Not shy." She glanced up the few inches to his face. "I'm never shy. I couldn't do my job if I was."

"Less social then," he amended.

"It's usually not personal."

"Personal?"

She thought about not replying but finally blurted out. "It was all that talk about my bones."

Why did I say that?

"I think you have very nice bones," he said. "Don't pay any attention to Ben. He thinks Kathy is attractive."

"She is attractive," she said. "Don't you think she's attractive?"

"Sure. I like her." He smiled. "I just don't want to dance with her."

The fiddle and banjo players were joined by a guitar player, and the trio played another slow song. Jack didn't seem in a hurry to get away from the dance, so Sarah stayed too.

Just one more dance, and I'll head back to the hotel.

"The barn looks good." Sarah searched for something to say.

"Yes. Just like a barn."

"It was a lot of work," she continued.

"It always is."

She sighed. "Why did you shave your beard and get all dressed up to build a barn?"

"I knew the dancing came after."

"So you wanted to dance with someone."

"With you." His gaze was steady on her face.

"Oh." She looked away, hoping to catch Kathy's eye so she could wave to her or something that would break the tension she was feeling. "That was really sweet of you."

"Sweet?" The word rolled off his tongue as though he had no experience with it. "I suppose you could say so. Is that what you really think?"

"I wonder how long this song is." She glanced at the musicians. "I'm not really familiar with the tune."

"I'll love you forever."

Sarah swallowed hard. "What?"

"The name of the song. *I'll Love You Forever.*"

She stared at him, suddenly wondering who he really was. She'd thought of him in so many different ways in the past few days—squatter, possible killer, crazy person, and maybe someone with PTSD. She had the urge to really figure out who Jack was and why he was there.

The tempo of the music changed again, back to the energetic dance that had the kids howling as they jumped down from the porch to join the party again.

"That's it for me," she said. "I'm exhausted. I have to go. Thanks for the dance."

"I'll see you to your car."

Sarah started to protest and tell him it wasn't necessary, but something about his voice and the determined way he'd said it made her believe he was going to do it whether she wanted him to or not.

And what could it hurt? It was barely dark and there were dozens of people in the yard. She wasn't afraid of him, just nervous. It was probably everything that had happened since she'd come back to Misty River. A walk with him to her car was nothing. She could handle it.

People called out to her as they saw her leave. A few thanked her for the pumpkins she'd brought that Mary and Gray were distributing to their workers as a way of saying thanks for their help with the barn. The ringing voices lasted halfway down the drive, almost until they'd reached her car.

"Have you ever really thought about keeping the farm and the pumpkin patch?" he asked. "You could claim the land for yourself."

"You mean so I'd be able to find the gold?" She made light of his question.

"You know what I mean. You loved it here as a child. Why would it be different now?"

"I'm not a kid anymore." She turned to him as they reached her car. "I don't want to swim in the river or pick pumpkins. That was a long time ago."

"I see."

"What about you, Jack? You're the one who needs to start looking forward. Monday, the land will belong to Leland Drake. He'll probably take down the house and barn. Think about what you're going to do. Kathy is offering you a job. Maybe you should take it."

He shrugged. "I guess we'll see what happens on Monday. Goodnight, Sarah. Thanks for the dance."

She hoped that didn't mean he had something else planned to mess things up.

Sarah watched him disappear into the shadows that surrounded the house and barn, skirting the edge of the lights and the party. She wanted to call him back and talk to him. There was more behind those blue eyes and wry smile. Part of her wanted to know what it was, to know the man himself.

Part of her said that was stupid.

She squared her shoulders as she got in the car, started the engine, and headed toward the hotel.

Chapter Thirteen

Sarah spent the rest of the evening washing clothes and taking care of other problems she'd put off. She decided to keep the clothes she'd taken from her mother's closet. They would be a souvenir of the last few days.

She called her mother to make sure she'd gotten home safely. She talked to her father who wanted to know why Sarah wasn't home already.

"Haven't you talked to Mom?" she asked.

"She told me some kind of story about the two of you getting drunk out there and not being sure about selling the property."

"She did?" That surprised Sarah. "I wasn't drunk. And I'm getting everything together to meet the buyer Monday and close the deal."

"It's about time," he said. "I don't know why your mother dropped the ball on this. If I'd known it was such a big deal, I would've handled it for her. I've never known her to be so emotional about selling a piece of land."

"It's not just a piece of land," Sarah argued. "This was her home. Grandma and Grandpa disappeared from here. It's a lot more than just a random tract of land. Of course she was going to be emotional."

"If Bess and Tommy wanted her to know where they'd gone, they would have told her."

The same argument he'd always made about their disappearance.

"It'll be over Monday," she told him. "No one will have to worry about it after that. I'll talk to you later, Dad."

She put the phone down with a shaky hand. She didn't like arguing with her father, especially about this. He'd been the big push behind getting it taken care of. It was different for her mother—she could see that now.

Sarah checked her email to take her mind off the sale of the property and everything else. Clare had sent her several messages about an upcoming fundraiser that she was worried about. The group holding the fundraiser had some very different opinions about state government than Clare's platform espoused. She was worried that some of her voters might take the event the wrong way.

It was a good opportunity to spend some time doing research for her job. It meant she didn't have time to think about Jack, George Burris, gold, or selling the property to Leland Drake.

An hour later, she reported her findings back to her boss—the fundraiser would be fine as long as she was careful with her remarks during the dinner.

After she was done with that, Sarah stared at the large screen TV in the hotel room. She didn't even realize that she hadn't turned it on for thirty minutes. At that point, she got up and walked around the room a few times.

Why did she feel bad for Jack? He had to know this day was going to come. He had a job offer. He didn't have to leave the area if he didn't want to. She didn't understand why he was so stubborn about it.

Some of her original thoughts about him surfaced—he had PTSD and couldn't face the real world, he only wanted to be there to guard the property from gold hunters, or he had other issues that he needed help with.

None of those answers went along with the man she was beginning to know. Everyone knew him and liked him. She could see how they treated him with respect, wanted his help, and valued his advice. She'd listened to him while he was talking to Gray about building the barn. He was well-spoken and clearheaded.

Possibly the biggest problem was that she couldn't get him out of her thoughts. The images of him with the huge beard that obscured his face and the ripped up, dirty clothes were directly opposite from the images of the man she'd danced with.

Why had he made that transformation? Was it something he did on a regular basis? Kathy and Ron had been surprised to see the change. There had been others there, too, who hadn't even recognized him.

So why had he done it?

His answer about being able to dance with her after the barn-raising made sleep impossible. Not knowing what was in his mind was driving her crazy.

Around midnight, exhausted from the hard work and getting up so early that morning, she climbed out of the hotel bed, got dressed, and headed back out to the farm. Maybe she could surprise him for a change. Maybe she could get some answers.

All the way to Misty River, she kept telling herself to go back. She didn't need to know what Jack was thinking. What difference did it make why he made himself presentable for a day? He might have thought he could convince her not to sell the land. Maybe he even thought she might find him attractive.

Do I find him attractive?

She hadn't been staring at his butt all day as Kathy had described physical attraction. Her marriage to Alan was finally over. She wasn't interested in having anyone in her life. Ron was just about having something to do until she went home. She knew without anyone telling her that Jack was more serious than that.

Sarah drove past the pumpkin patch sign that had been hanging on one chain. The car headlights picked up the repair that had been done on it. It looked new. Someone had painstakingly repainted it and hung it again.

Jack.

He didn't believe her when she said she wasn't staying. He still thought he could convince her to save the farm. She had to find a way to make him understand that this wasn't the life she wanted. Even though she'd thought she'd made it clear, there had to be something more that she could say.

She drove the car into the dark drive and parked. Jack would be in the barn. The chances were good that he wouldn't be looking for her and not expecting her back that night.

Before she left the car—eager to sneak up on him—the intelligent, reasoning part of her brain told her to leave. There were no answers here that she really wanted. She had to stay on track until Monday when she could hand over the land to Leland Drake and go home.

But something uncontrollable in her heart whispered, *stay*.

Sarah had rarely ever allowed her heart to dictate to her brain. She'd always known what she wanted and what she had to do to get it. She'd never had time for anyone in her life who wasn't as disciplined and didn't know what he wanted. Alan was even more like her—driven and ambitious.

What am I looking for, a roll in the hay with the first boy who ever kissed me? Is that what this is about?

If she wanted to have a short fling with a man, Ron would certainly be her best bet. If not him, then a dozen other men that she knew back home. It wouldn't be a man who lived in a barn and only cleaned up every few years when he went to a dance.

But even as she argued with herself, she got out of the car and then steadily passed the quiet house, walking toward the barn. There was a thin sliver of light coming from under the barn door as she approached.

She knew Jack was in there. The tractor he'd brought back was outside. She put her hand on the rough wood.

One last chance to leave before he sees you. You could still go back to the hotel without him ever knowing.

Her rapidly beating heart won the argument. She pushed open the barn door with a trembling hand. The mother cat glanced up to see what was going on, her babies sleeping around her. The light had been coming from a lamp over the rough bed on the far side of the barn from where she stood.

Two dark figures were lying on the hay-covered floor. A large gun was between them.

"Jack!"

Chapter Fourteen

Sarah ran unerringly toward him. He wasn't moving. The dim light showed her an ugly, red wound on his forehead.

She went to the old sink where her grandfather used to clean up before he went inside. There was a clean t-shirt hanging there. She grabbed it and got it wet before she went back to him.

The cold water revived him as she put part of the wet shirt on his face and dabbed at the blood.

"Sarah?" His eyes barely opened. "What are you doing here?"

"I don't know." She moved the wet cloth so she could get a better look at the wound. "That's going to need stitches."

He groaned and glanced around. "What happened?"

"I just got here. And there's someone else."

"Get behind me." He tried to sit up and couldn't do it.

"Don't worry. He's not moving either. Can't you remember?"

Jack finally sat up slowly. "I remember. I heard a noise and went to check on it."

"Whoever it was tried to kill you." Her hands were freezing from the cold water. "Hold this. I'll check on the other guy."

"Be careful," he whispered. "Just because he's not moving doesn't mean he's not dangerous."

She got up and found a rough piece of wood on the floor. She wasn't sure if she could swing it hard enough to stop someone from killing her, but the man on the other side of the room was still not moving. The gun was between them. She could pick it up on the way.

Half crouching as she went toward him, her steps were light and careful. If he was unconscious, she didn't want to wake him. If it was some gold hunter who thought he could take on Jack, he'd make mincemeat out of her.

"Sarah." Jack's tone was a warning.

She put her hand on the gun and picked it up. "I've got it. I'm not sure what to do with it. It's so big."

"You use it just like any other gun," he recommended. "Bring it to me."

"He's right here. I might as well see who it is. I've got the gun. He doesn't know I don't know how to shoot it."

"Except that you just told him."

Sarah glanced back at Jack for an instant before moving toward the other man on the floor. She nudged him with the end of the rifle.

"Who is it?"

"I'm not sure. I think he's badly hurt. But I can't see his face."

Jack got up slowly and put his hands against the other man's throat. The dim light barely illuminated Leland Drake's open eyes. "He's gone."

"Leland?" Sarah asked. "Why would he be out here?"

"Let me see that rifle." He took it from her and

examined it. "That's what I thought."

"What?"

"It's a Ruger 357. Probably the same gun that killed George Burris."

"So Leland killed George?"

"I seriously doubt it. But it looks like someone wants people to think I did."

"That's crazy! You—"

She'd barely spoken the words when a dozen sheriff's deputies stormed in through the open barn door. Large flashlight beams played over Jack, Sarah, and Leland.

"Are you all right, Ms. Tucker?" one of the deputies asked.

Sarah recognized him from the investigation into George's death. "I'm fine. I'm so glad you're here. Leland Drake is dead."

"We know," he said. "We got a tip. Sheriff Morgan is on his way. Just come toward us. You'll be okay."

"But I—"

"Go on, Sarah," Jack said.

She suddenly understood what the deputy was saying. "Oh. No—you have it wrong. Jack isn't trying to hurt me. When I got here, he was unconscious too. I think Leland tried to kill him."

"Please come this way, Ms. Tucker." The deputy put out his hand to guide her but never lowered his gun from Jack's face. "We'll settle this when we know you're safe."

"It's okay," Jack said quietly. "Go with him. You'll be fine."

"They think you killed Leland," she explained as though he was a child who didn't understand. "You're hurt. You need to go to the hospital."

"I'm fine," he said. "Please just go with him, and we'll sort it out when the sheriff gets here."

"All right." She finally gave up and defiantly marched across the room to the line of deputies. "But if he dies, I'm going to bring a criminal lawsuit against all of you!"

Jack put down the rifle and held his hands in the air.

"Lie down on the floor," the deputy ordered. "Put your hands behind your back."

Sheriff Morgan seemed to come out of nowhere. "What a mess! What happened here?"

"What did your tipster tell you?" Jack responded as the deputy cuffed him.

"Someone called and said that he heard gunfire back here after seeing you and Leland arguing down by the road." Sheriff Morgan put his hands on his narrow hips. "Is that true?"

"No, it's not true," Sarah said. "Leland attacked Jack. They were both out cold when I got here."

"Except Leland is dead." The sheriff crouched beside the man's body.

"Jack needs an ambulance," she repeated. "Look at his head."

The sheriff glanced at the deep gash on Jack's head as the deputy helped him to his feet.

"Yeah, I think that probably needs looking at. We'll take care of it, Ms. Tucker. Don't you worry."

She got in front of the deputy who was starting to lead Jack out of the barn. "I am worried about it. Jack didn't kill Leland. I can't believe you think he did."

Sheriff Morgan nodded. "Believe me, we'll give him every benefit of the doubt, but right now I gotta tell you—it's not looking good."

"It's okay," Jack told her. "You have to let the process work. I shouldn't have to tell you that."

Sarah still wasn't happy with the idea that they were arresting the wrong man. She walked out of the barn with them as they headed toward several cars—lights flashing—and put Jack in the backseat of one of them.

Kathy drove up, braking fast as she left her pickup in the street and ran to where Sarah was standing. "What happened? I heard on the police scanner that someone else was killed here."

"Leland Drake," Sarah told her. "And they're arresting Jack for it."

"What? Why?"

"We're going to need a bail bondsman."

"I know somebody. Ben has a brother that does that work. Want me to give him a call?"

"Yes, please. Tell him I'll meet him at the county jail. Thanks, Kathy."

Sarah ran to her car. Jack wasn't staying in custody one minute longer than was necessary.

"Hey!" Kathy called. "You want me to go with you?"

"It's okay. I know how to handle this."

Thinking carefully about her next actions, Sarah drove quickly through the night back to her hotel room to change clothes and then on to get Jack out of jail.

She believed his story and knew she could help him. The situation was continuing to escalate, drawing her in deeper. First George's death—now Leland's. She wasn't going to be able to sell the land on Monday, but she also couldn't go home.

The sheriff's office was next to the county jail. The office was busy, but the jail looked quiet and dark. Sarah walked up the sidewalk to the sheriff's office, hoping Jack hadn't been transferred next door as yet. The chances were good that it would take longer to process him. He might not get a bail hearing until the next day—unless she pushed the matter.

Sarah had done similar things for one of Clare's sons who had a habit of getting into trouble. It was her job to make sure he was taken care of before the press figured out what was going on. The charges were never anything like murder. Once he'd taken someone's car out joy riding, and another time he'd been caught trespassing at a new business in Richmond that he thought shouldn't be there.

Of course Clare had a PR person who smoothed everything over as Sarah worked behind the scenes. She was on her own with Jack.

She asked for Sheriff Morgan at the front desk. The deputy went to get him. When the sheriff showed up, he ushered her back to a small office.

"What can I do for you, Ms. Tucker?"

"I want to speak to my client." She had a white-knuckled death-grip on her handbag. This was personal. She didn't want to let Jack down. But that made her nervous in a way that she never was when it was for someone else's benefit.

"Why are you here? It hasn't been that long that you thought Jack might've killed your grandparents and George. Now you're all hopped up to get him out of jail. Why the turn around?"

"I don't have to tell you that, Sheriff Morgan. Where's Jack?"

"You don't even know his last name, do you?"

Sarah raised her head and stuck out her chin defiantly. "I will as soon as you show me the arrest warrant."

He shook his head. "All right. If you say he's your client, he's your client."

She relaxed a little. "Let me ask you why you suddenly think Jack is guilty of killing someone. All this time you were sure he'd never do such a thing."

"I have to admit that I wouldn't have thought it, but Jack might be getting desperate. First it was the treasure hunters, and now you're selling the land for the Blue Way project. He's seeing his home ripped away from him. He has nowhere to go and nothing to do. He might be willing to kill to prevent the sale from happening. I know he hired Trent to slow you down."

"Seriously?" She stared at him. "If Jack wanted to keep anything from happening to the land, all he had to do was kill me. Why take the circle route when he could weed out the problem at the root?"

He sipped coffee from his cup. "Don't think I haven't asked myself the same question. Maybe he thought killing you would be too obvious. But if enough bad stuff happened surrounding the sale, you might go away and forget the place is here for another twenty years."

"And what did the caller say who tipped you that Jack and Leland were fighting in the driveway?"

He got to his feet and towered over her. "I don't have to share that information right now. That will be up to the DA. But when someone tells us two men are fighting, and we come out to find one man dead and the other standing over him with the murder weapon in his hands, that makes a compelling argument."

"You're wrong," she argued. "Where's Jack?"

"You're sure you want to go through with this?"

Sarah got to her feet and fixed him with one of her most intimidating stares. "Right now."

Chapter Fifteen

The sheriff shrugged and told her to wait where she was. A few minutes later, Ron and the deputy who'd been at the barn, led Jack into the room and cuffed him to the table.

"I'm sorry about this," Ron muttered. "I hope we can still have lunch."

She told him that was fine, barely hearing what he said. When he was gone and the door had closed behind him, she faced her client across the table.

"You shouldn't be here," he said.

"Neither should you. Do you remember anything about what happened at the barn?"

"I don't need a lawyer."

"Too bad. You've already got one." She repeated her question.

"I told you what I remember. I can handle this. Maybe you should talk to Mace. I think he has a few other buyers waiting in the wings. You don't want to lose another day without a sale."

"Why are you acting this way? These are serious charges, and for some reason, the sheriff isn't on your side anymore. Let's start from the beginning and figure out what really happened."

He wouldn't make eye contact. "You can't help me."

She wanted to grab him and shake him. "Yes, I can. I do things like this all the time. I'll get you out on bond, and we can decide what to do from there."

"No. Don't do anything else that might come back on you." Jack frowned. "I don't need you. Go back to Richmond."

"Why are you doing this? Let me help."

"No." He called for the deputy, who was standing outside the door. "I'm ready to go back."

Sarah watched him leave. What was wrong with him? A sane person in his position should be thrilled to have representation. She walked out behind him and located the sheriff.

"You haven't done anything for that gash in his head yet. I don't know if he's said something to you, but I plan to file a legal document that he was incapacitated and didn't know what he was saying when you found him at the barn."

Sheriff Morgan leaned back in his chair and chuckled. "Can't take rejection, huh? Yeah. He told me he didn't want to see you. I can't think why. What have you two been doing out there that made you come in here guns blazing and Jack didn't want to see your face?"

"Just take care of him," she warned. "You know he's not guilty of killing Leland."

"Do I?"

"I think you do. I've listened to your impassioned 'Jack is a good guy' talks the last few days. I understand that you can't ignore the evidence at this point, but we both know he didn't do it."

"You should go on back to your hotel and get some sleep. What were you doing out there anyway?"

"None of your business. I'll be back in the morning."

Sarah heard him laughing as she walked out the door.

Kathy was waiting outside with Ben and his brother. Sarah told the rough-looking bail bondsman what her limits were for cash bail and that she would put up her property, if necessary, to get Jack out of jail.

Ben's brother had her sign some forms. She gave him her information, and he told her he'd be in touch as soon as he heard about the bond hearing.

"How's Jack doing?" Kathy asked after Ben and his brother had left.

"You know any place around here to get a decent cup of coffee?" Sarah yawned. "I think it's going to be a long night."

The two women ended up at a diner not far from the sheriff's office. There were several off-duty deputies enjoying homemade cinnamon rolls and coffee when they walked in. One of them was the deputy who'd arrested Jack. He nodded when he saw Sarah. She looked away.

The waitress put the women at a booth that faced the highway. They talked about what Sarah knew about Leland's death and Jack's arrest.

"Somebody is setting him up," Kathy said after their coffee had arrived. She also asked for a piece of lemon meringue pie that had been in a glass case on the counter. "Are you sure you don't want something to eat?"

"I can't even think about eating right now."

"Because it's so early in the morning or because Jack is in trouble?"

"Both." Sarah shook her head. "I barely know Jack. Like the sheriff said—I don't even know his last name. I assume he has one."

Kathy shrugged as she dug into her pie. "I've never heard it. Everybody calls him Jack. But I'm sure you're right. I guess you'll know everything about him if you bail him out. Are you really going to do it?"

"I can't let him stay in there. Who knows when the trial

will come up? He doesn't want me to represent him, but I don't care."

"That's just pride talking," Kathy said. "He feels stupid that you have to help him. I think he likes being all secretive and everything. That's why he had the beard and wears the old rags. Except with you—care to guess why he changed his appearance?"

"No." Sarah sighed, thinking about the feelings that had brought her out in the middle of the night to talk to him. "He's going to be my client. I'm only supposed to find ways to prove he's innocent. Nothing else matters."

Kathy licked her fork, cleaning the meringue from it. "Like that, is it? That's what I thought when I saw the two of you dancing. You make a cute couple."

Sarah drank some coffee and ignored her romantic fancies.

"Who do you think snitched on Jack to set him up?" Kathy changed the subject.

"Probably whoever killed George Burris and Leland. I'm guessing both men were killed by the same rifle, the Ruger 357. Jack was a perfect patsy."

"That Ruger is hard to find. I don't think I know anybody who has one. But I could ask around and see who sells them locally."

"Thanks. That might be a big help."

"You don't think Jack did it, right?" Kathy demanded. "You wouldn't go through all this trouble for him just because you like him, would you?"

"No. Of course not. Jack is okay, but defending him against murder is different. I wouldn't get him out on bond if I thought he was guilty, no matter how I feel about him personally."

"But you do like him. Romantically, I mean."

"I don't even know him," Sarah blustered. "Can we stick to saving his life?"

Kathy giggled. "It's okay with me. Don't worry. I won't tell anyone."

They talked over a dozen cups of coffee before Kathy had to go home and get started on her chores.

Sarah didn't want to drive to the hotel and back again. Instead she drove back to the sheriff's office and wrote a carefully worded text to her mother and Clare about what had happened. She knew she wouldn't hear back from either of them until later in the day. She sat in her car and watched the sunrise. Her life felt like it was spiraling out of control.

A tapping on her window, accompanied by her phone buzzing, woke her at seven-thirty. It was finally light outside. She realized she'd fallen asleep. Yawning, she opened the window to a woman from the sheriff's department telling her that she couldn't sleep in the parking lot.

The phone call was from Ben's brother. They were holding a bond hearing for Jack at eight. Everything was arranged, but Jack was being difficult.

"He says he wants to stay in jail," Ben's brother said. "I'll let you handle that."

"Thanks."

Jack's bail was high because the court considered him to be a homeless person with no guarantee that he wouldn't run as soon as he was released. Sarah had to use the farm as collateral to secure his bond.

Once they were in the courtroom, she stepped up with her name and credentials to declare that she was representing him. She was glad to see that he had a large white bandage on his forehead. She hoped being treated for the wound helped get his mind together.

"In the matter of Jack Richard Collins." The bailiff stated the case for the judge.

Collins. Sarah filed that information away in her brain. *Jack Collins.*

"How do you plead, Mr. Collins?" the judge asked impatiently.

"Sarah Tucker for the defense, Your Honor. My client pleads not guilty." She got her head in the game. Jack was quiet and didn't disagree with her.

"ADA Reynolds," the judge proceeded. "What are you asking as bail?"

"We're asking five-hundred-thousand dollars, Your Honor, as we consider the defendant to be a flight risk."

Sarah tried to talk him down. The bail was too high—Jack had lived in the community for many years, even if he didn't currently have a home address. It didn't work.

Ben's brother assured the court that bail had been posted. The judge set a court date and banged her gavel to announce the proceeding was finished.

They walked out of the courtroom, and Ben's brother warned Jack not to run. "I have a reputation. Nobody gets away from me."

"He's not going anywhere," Sarah replied. "Thanks for your help."

Ben's brother walked away toward his pickup that was parked on the side of the courthouse. Sarah had a problem opening the doors to her rental car with the key fob but finally managed to get it right. She and Jack got in the car.

"I really don't like that man," Jack said. "The next time I'm in jail for killing someone, could you find someone else?"

Sarah laughed until tears came to her eyes. "So it's Jack Collins, huh?"

"That's right." He looked down at his hands that had only been out of cuffs for a few minutes. "Thanks. You shouldn't have done it. But thanks."

"You couldn't just stay in there." She started the car. "I need your help to find the real killer."

"And you're convinced that isn't me?"

"Yes. Was there ever any doubt?"

Sarah started to pull out of the parking lot, and he put his hand on hers.

"How could there not be some doubt? You barely know me."

"I've been listening to everyone sing your praises since I got here. They can't all be wrong. Let's get something to eat.

I know a diner with a good cup of coffee and really thick lemon meringue pie."

"Wherever you want to go. You paid for me. I'm all yours."

He moved his hand so she could turn the steering wheel. She glanced at him uneasily and then left the courthouse.

Chapter Sixteen

Over breakfast with a loud group of truckers surrounding them at the diner, Sarah and Jack talked about what had happened at the barn. Unfortunately there wasn't much to say—he only heard a noise before he was knocked unconscious and came to when she got there.

"My fingerprints are going to be all over that rifle." He'd already polished off three eggs, bacon, biscuits, coffee, and orange juice.

"We have to think about who else might want George and Leland dead." She'd watched him eat after barely making it through some toast and fruit. The lemon meringue pie was in a to-go box. "It has to involve the land, right? It has to be about the gold."

"Or someone besides me doesn't want you to sell it."

"I understand your reasoning. I can't imagine why anyone else wouldn't want me to sell."

"Keep an eye on who Mace presents next as a potential

buyer. It might be a treasure hunter."

The pretty waitress smiled at Jack as she poured him more coffee and asked if he needed anything else.

"You mean someone who killed Leland to keep him from getting the land, and maybe killed George before he had a chance to convince me to sell it to him."

"I think you'd make a good private detective," Jack observed. "Maybe you've missed your calling."

"I don't think so. I'm not really good with emergencies." She studied his face. "Do you think this could have something to do with my grandparents?"

"It's possible, I suppose, but with the killer out there right now, he would've waited a long time to get this done. No one has been able to access the land since I got back."

"Okay. So probably not. It would've been nice to wrap the whole thing up."

"You'll figure that out, too, someday. I'm sure the answer is out there."

She took a deep breath and restructured her thoughts. "How's your head?"

"Not as bad as it looks." He touched it. "It only took ten stitches."

"Oh! Is that all?"

He nodded. "I've had worse."

They drove back to the farm after breakfast. Sarah thought it would be good if they could take another look at the barn. But there was a crime scene van in the driveway and a deputy stationed outside the door as the team worked inside to find trace evidence.

Sarah and Jack went back to the house. She wasn't sure what to do next. They sat on the stairs where she'd been with her mother and stared out at the acres of land stretched before them.

"Are we going to have to wait to do something until Mace finds out about Leland's death and calls me with another buyer?" she asked impatiently.

"I think that's what you should do. It's not a good idea

for you to get involved investigating a killer. You don't have the skills for it."

"And you do? I think it would involve more than driving a tractor or putting up a barn."

"I think I could manage."

"I think I could too. I'm going to hire a private detective. My mother and I talked about finding one to search for my grandparents again anyway. He might as well see if he can find out who killed George and Leland too."

"There aren't many private investigators out here. Maybe you should think about going back to Richmond and finding one."

She put her arms around her knees as she drew them to her chest. "I get the feeling that you want to get rid of me."

"It would be safer for you."

"And make it easier for you to skip out on your bail. I'm not leaving until this is over." Sarah glanced at the house. "I guess I'd better get the water turned on. I can give up my hotel room and stay here. It would make more sense."

"Is there anything I could say to change your mind?" he asked. "It could be dangerous for you."

"No. I guess I either need to get my pistol back from the sheriff or get a bigger gun. I'm not going anywhere."

He shook his head. "I knew you were going to be stubborn the minute I saw you."

"You mean sixteen years ago when I got locked in the springhouse and you helped me get out?"

"No." He smiled slowly. "When you were tangled in that rosebush and couldn't stay still long enough to get yourself free. I can see you haven't changed."

Sarah got to her feet. "I'll open the windows and air out the house. I wish I could do something about the living room. It's kind of creepy the way it is with the big hole cut out of the carpet where George died."

"I'm sure you'll think of something."

She spent the next two hours going through the house. She decided to sleep in her mother's old room. It was smaller than the one her grandparents had shared, but she couldn't bring herself to stay in there.

Because the kitchen and the rest of the house had been left alone, there were plenty of pots and pans, a toaster, dishes and other necessities that she wouldn't have to purchase.

Sarah had a good time looking through her grandmother's old cookbooks, many of the recipes in her own hand. Some of the recipes were complicated but some even she could do. She was going to take them home with her when she left, no matter what.

Once the water was on, she'd be fine. She supposed she'd have to figure out who she'd need to pay in town the next day. Maybe there was a website.

Jack rapped at the back door and then walked into the kitchen. "Try the water."

"What? Did you tap in illegally or something? I can wait to do it the right way."

He walked past her and turned on the faucet at the kitchen sink. Slightly brown water gushed out. "Where did you think it came from? The pump was turned off so the pipes wouldn't freeze in the winter."

"That's great. I thought there was only the hand pump in back. Thanks."

"I have an idea about the living room floor too."

She followed him out of the kitchen. "Really?"

"We can move the furniture out of here and pull up the rest of the carpet. The floor is oak under it. Once you clean it up, it will look great. It won't remind you of George anymore."

"I think it might take more than that for me to forget there was a dead body in here. But that's a good idea. Thanks."

"I'll help you."

For the next hour they worked in companionable silence. They moved the furniture into the kitchen. Sarah smoothed her hand over the lace doilies on the arms of the sofa and chairs. Her grandmother had made these after learning to tat from her great-grandmother. Bess had tried to teach her when she was about ten, but Sarah didn't have the patience for it. Now she wished she would've learned.

Jack pulled up the carpet and took it outside. Sarah started scrubbing the floor with wood soap. She stopped long enough to inhale the smell of lemon oil and then put her back into the task. She glanced up to see Jack working from the other side. They met in the middle and backed out of the room.

The windows had been open while they'd worked. Only one pane of glass had shattered with the impact of the bullet. The rest were intact. Jack had cut a piece of cardboard to close that gap.

Sarah smiled at it. Leave it to a man to think he could just stuff a piece of cardboard in the hole.

"I can get a piece of glass for it later," he said as though he was reading her mind.

"That's fine. Thanks for your help. I should make Mace replace it anyway. He can bill me after he sells the house."

Her cell phone rang. It was Ron asking when he could pick her up for lunch. She glanced at the time. It was already after noon. She'd forgotten her promise to him.

"I can be ready in a few minutes," she told him. "Thanks."

"Broadwell?" Jack asked when she'd finished the call.

"Yes. I guess I should go." She felt guilty not even offering him lunch for his trouble, but there was no food in the house. "Let me give you something for all you've done." She grabbed her handbag.

"No, thanks."

She hunted through it, trying to find some cash. She finally fished out a twenty and looked up, but he was gone. "Jack?" she yelled. "Don't be stupid. You worked hard for it."

There was no response. He was probably halfway to the barn. She put the twenty on the table with a note that he should take it. She wished she had more, but she didn't carry much cash with her.

Sarah went upstairs to find something else to wear. It only took a few minutes to find a cute blue sundress. Her younger mother had good taste in clothes. It wasn't exactly sundress weather, but it was still warm enough for the shorter skirt and cap sleeves. Her mother's old sandals barely fit and were kind of ratty, but they would have to do.

She brushed her hair and put on some lipstick. Her face was even pinker from the sun yesterday. If she was here much longer, her face would be completely covered by freckles as her grandmother's had been.

Before she could talk herself out of going, she went downstairs and out the door to meet him. The mother cat and her kittens were outside on the porch in the sun. She stroked their warm bodies and laughed as the kittens kept pushing each other out of place as they tried to nurse.

The barn still had yellow tape across the door. The deputy and crime scene people were gone, but Jack wouldn't be able to sleep there tonight.

She needed to talk to him about taking one of the other bedrooms in the house. Since he maintained it, he might as well get some use out of it. There was no reason for him to sleep in the barn at all—at least until after the house was sold. It could be a while before another offer came around to sell the place after the bad publicity.

Ron honked the horn in the driveway. She carefully walked around the corner of the house, avoiding the rosebush, and waved to him.

He wasn't driving a sheriff's car, which was nice. He had an older Chevy that he was wiping down as she got there. "I restored this Impala. I've been working on it since I was a kid. My granddad gave it to me."

Sarah smoothed her hand over the glossy, burgundy finish. "It's very nice." She knew nothing about cars except how to drive them. It made her feel girly to admit it, so she walked around the car trying to think of something good to say about it. "You've done a great job on it."

"Thanks. Hop in. We're going someplace special."

Since the only place in town was the Burger Shack, Sarah assumed that meant they were going to the next town over. Silver Springs was bigger than Misty River and actually had a few restaurants and a grocery store.

She was right. Ron whizzed past the town line and pulled up in front of a newer restaurant that boasted all its food was served family-style. It smelled like fried chicken, and there were plenty of cars outside. She guessed that meant family-style was a good thing.

"My old buddy from school owns this place. He bought it from the people who were retiring. You'll love it." He put his arm around her as they walked inside.

She didn't say anything about it or try to move away. He was probably that kind of person—huggy and touchy—like Kathy.

The restaurant was packed. They were seated right away at a corner table. Ron's friend came out to talk to them for a few minutes, and then the salad was served.

Family-style apparently meant large amounts of food served in big bowls, she realized, as a huge bowl of salad was followed by an even bigger basket of warm sourdough bread.

Ron was pushed tightly up against her on one side of the booth, even though there was plenty of room to scoot over or go to the other side. His hand kept drifting to her bare knee and higher. Sarah didn't think of herself as a prude, but she also didn't feel she wanted to know him that well. This was just supposed to be something to fill her Sunday.

They each got plates. He insisted on serving her, heaping her plate with a mound of salad she could never eat.

"So what is Sarah Tucker all about?" He broke apart some bread and handed her a piece.

She shook her head. "No, thanks. I guess I'm a lawyer from Richmond who needs to sell the family farm so I can go back home."

"You're a lawyer? That's how you got Jack out of jail so

fast." He nodded. "I kind of think he did it. Everyone knows he's been living off the fat of the land out there, trying to find the gold. He might even be responsible for what happened to your grandparents. Have you thought about that?"

Chapter Seventeen

Sarah admitted that she'd thought about all of it. "But I don't think Jack's a killer."

"You can't ever tell until you're standing there and he's got a gun aimed at you."

The next course, which was fried chicken and mashed potatoes, was served with corn on the cob. Ron filled a plate for her and gave himself twice as much.

"What about you?" she asked. "What kind of things do you like to do?"

"I like hunting and fishing. I watch some NASCAR. Mostly being a deputy means being on call twenty-four/seven. I don't have much time to go out. My parents still live in Misty River. I hope to die there and be buried right alongside them."

"That sounds interesting." She slid over a little, hoping he would get the point. "It must be a difficult job being a deputy."

"Not so much. One day, I'm gonna take Sheriff Morgan's place." He grinned. "Then it'll be Sheriff Broadwell for about twenty years until I retire."

"I guess you've got it all planned out." Sarah smiled and ate some chicken. The crust on the outside was crispy, the inside tender and delicious. "This is really good."

"I knew you'd like it. You're a down-home girl. Stay here a few years, and you'll figure it out for yourself."

"Thanks, but I have a life to get back to. It's beautiful here. Sometimes I wish I could stay."

"What's stopping you? Jack? I could run him out of there this afternoon."

Ron sounded so sincere that she paused. She didn't want him to hurt Jack. "That's not what's stopping me from living here. He doesn't bother me, and he's been a big help."

"If you don't count the two murders he's committed trying to keep you from selling the land. I'm telling you for your own good. He'd do anything to stay out there so he can keep looking for the gold. What do you think he's been doing out there all these years? Waiting for Tommy and Bess to come home?"

She thought about what he said, even though the conversation changed to events he thought were important to Misty River. His friend came back out to ask them if they'd enjoyed the meal. Sarah complimented his cook. She'd barely been able to touch the banana pudding or peanut butter pie that was for dessert, but her date had eaten both their shares.

The restaurant was still busy when they left. Ron took her by the river, pointing out the Blue Way Trail that would follow it.

"I don't know what Leland's son will do now that his old man is gone. He might not be interested in your property or even doing the Blue Way on his own. I think that was all Leland's idea. He was always interested in trying to grow the town. He's a big loss to us all. Jack has a lot to answer for."

"You know, we still consider people innocent until

proven guilty," she snapped. "Jack will have his day in court, but I don't think they'll convict him of anything. I know he didn't kill George Burris. I was there when it happened."

"No offense, but things aren't always what they seem. You trust Jack because your grandparents did, even though that may have cost them their lives."

Sarah didn't argue with him as they wandered along the river path. The mist that the river was famous for was rising. Legends said the mist meant all kinds of things. Her grandfather had told her that the mist meant the river had healing properties. Her grandmother said it meant that it was good for fishing.

"You could keep the property," Ron said. "You could hire a manager to set things up so it could still connect to the Blue Way. That way it would stay in your family, and you'd get the money too."

"I don't think the rest of my family would go along with that. They just want to get rid of it."

But she wasn't sure of that anymore. Her mother had briefly faltered in her decision to sell. Dusty probably didn't care either way—he didn't need the money. As long as he didn't have to do anything with the property, he'd probably be fine with keeping it.

They got back to her house later than she'd expected. Despite their disagreements on a few subjects, she'd had a good time. Ron was a little too hands-on for her, but he'd been an interesting companion.

"Well, this is me," she said with a smile. "I had a good time. Thanks for taking me out."

He got out of the car and wrapped his arms around her. "Come on. Let's go inside for a while. Kids call it the ghost house since no one has lived here for so long. Everyone sneaks into the patch to grab a pumpkin, but they're careful not to get too close to the house."

"I would've thought you'd seen enough of it while you were investigating the shooting."

"I haven't been upstairs." He grinned. "I wouldn't mind

seeing that part."

Sarah got cold feet. "Maybe that's not such a great idea right now. The house is a mess after sitting empty for so long. There's no running water. Maybe some other time."

"I understand. That's okay. Maybe you'd like to take a look at *my* place instead."

"Thanks, but I'm really tired. I don't think I've ever worked as hard as I did yesterday. But thanks again for dinner."

He pulled her tightly to him and pushed his mouth against hers, scrubbing it back and forth over her lips. Sarah politely waited for him to finish before she thanked him again and hurried around the back of the house. She took a deep breath as she stood beside the old rosebush.

"That bad, huh?"

She jumped back and realized that her dress was caught in the thorns.

"Or that good?"

Sarah tried to reach around and untangle the back of her dress from the large thorns. "I can't believe you were spying on us."

"Not much else to do."

"I knew you should've taken the job that Kathy and Ben offered." A second vine got caught on her dress. She huffed loudly in frustration. So much for being an adult and not getting caught in the roses.

Jack moved closer to her. "Stand still. You're only making it worse."

She stood still while he reached his hand around her waist to free her dress from the thorns. It was embarrassing, but it worked. *If I do stay here, I'm cutting this thing down to the ground!*

"There you go."

Sarah took a quick step forward before he moved out of the way and ended up very close to him. She could smell the soap he used and heard his quick intake of breath.

"As much fun as it looks like you two are having,"

Sheriff Morgan said, "I need to have a few words with Jack in private."

Jack moved, and Sarah got away from the roses.

She realized that the sheriff must have sneaked in after her. "Whatever you have to say to him, you can say to me too. I represent him."

"It's okay," Jack said. "We'll be right back."

"I can't help if you exclude me and talk to him on your own," she yelled after them as they walked toward the barn.

Neither one of them turned back. Sarah decided Jack was on his own after he'd ignored her warning. She went inside and found a pencil and paper. She was going to need some supplies and the rest of her things from the hotel. She made a list of basic foods that would be easy to eat without a microwave. There were also necessities like toilet paper and dish soap. She quickly added other cleaning products to her list.

She was finishing her list, after taking down some of her grandmother's china, when Sheriff Morgan came in. She'd left the door open to catch the cool breezes. It was warm and there was no air conditioning in the house. There never had been—her grandmother had hated it.

"Ms. Tucker." He nodded as he sat at the table with her. "Looks like you're staying longer than you planned."

"I'm sure you know that things have come up," she said.

"Just a bit of friendly advice."

Sarah looked up from her list and noticed the twenty-dollar bill still on the table.

"About Jack—this might not be a good time to get involved with him."

Her face got hot as she realized what he'd thought was going on by the rose bush. She didn't enlighten him. It was none of his business.

"Sometimes people, like yourself, get out of their natural element and can't figure how to get back."

"Thanks, Sheriff. But I think I know my way home."

"Like I said, just some friendly advice. I know you're

recently divorced."

Really? His investigation into her background was thorough.

"I'm recently divorced, and you know what they say about once bitten. I'm not in the market for a romance."

"I've said what I have to say." He got up, hat in hand. "Keep an eye out. This thing might not be over, whatever it is. I'd hate to see you get caught in the crossfire."

"I thought you had it all figured out? Isn't Jack guilty of killing both men?"

"I didn't say that I was done poking around. We know from ballistics that the 357 rifle we found in the barn is guilty of killing George and Leland. Jack makes the best suspect right now. That doesn't mean it's over. But you take care, Ms. Tucker."

He nodded again and left the way he'd come. She sighed and finished her list listening to the birds calling outside from the oak tree behind the house. Her grandfather had been an avid bird watcher, identifying the different bird calls for her.

Finally rousing herself enough to go shopping and check out of the hotel, Sarah took a peek in the living room. While she was gone with Ron, Jack had moved the furniture back and even added a small vase of daisies to the old coffee table.

"What do you think?" he asked from behind her.

"I think I should tie a bell around your neck. And the living room looks great. I can't quite envision George's dead body there anymore. Thanks."

"My pleasure." He turned to leave.

"Wait a minute. I'm going to check out at the hotel and pick up some supplies for the next few days. Can I get something for you since you wouldn't take money for helping me?"

"I owe you a lot more than twenty dollars for getting me out of jail."

"But you can't go on living this way. You aren't going to be able to stay here much longer. You turned down Kathy's job. You won't take my money. How are you going to survive?"

He smiled. "You know, it's been a long time since someone worried about me. But you don't have to. I'll be fine. And I don't particularly need anything."

"Ron said you've been here the last sixteen years searching for the gold. He said you'll do anything to keep me from selling the land so you can keep looking."

"You believe that?"

"It makes sense. I guess that's why Sheriff Morgan arrested you and charged you with murder. You need a better story. You need an alibi."

"Well, first if I'd been out here digging holes for the last sixteen years, I think you'd have noticed. And I don't have a better story. This is it. Maybe you should call Ron and tell him so he doesn't have to worry about me either."

"Okay. Maybe I put that the wrong way." Sarah tried to amend her words. Maybe she wouldn't have noticed before, but now she recognized that she'd hurt his feelings—or his pride. She wasn't sure which. "I don't believe you killed anyone. I don't think you've been looking for gold, or you probably would've found it."

"Thanks." He hadn't turned back to face her, perched in the doorway as though he was ready to run.

"But I don't know if a jury is going to believe it."

"It won't come to that."

"Please think about your future. It's coming faster than you realize."

He left without another word. She'd meant to ask him if he wanted to spend the night in the house since he couldn't go in the barn, but there hadn't been time for it.

Her phone rang. It was Mace. "I have another interested buyer for the property. He'd like to meet with you tomorrow. What time is good for you?"

Chapter Eighteen

Sarah agreed to meet with Mace's buyer at noon. She had to go to the courthouse first and pick up a copy of the deed. Her mother had faxed her grandparents' death certificate to her at the real estate office. That made it easier for her to get everything together for the sale.

There was one problem that she couldn't think of a way around—she'd put up the property for Jack's bond. She couldn't sell it until he appeared in court. She thought she could meet with the buyer and explain the situation. If he was still interested, they could talk further, and she could set up a later date for sale.

Jack wasn't going to run, but she couldn't convince a judge or Ben's bail-bondsman brother of it. She didn't even try. If she had an agreement from the buyer, she could sign the papers before the trial, and when the bond was vacated, the buyer would be notified.

With all of that working in her head, Sarah packed up

her things at the hotel and checked out. She went to a grocery store and filled a cart with her purchases, some that were not the necessities she'd promised herself she was going to buy. She spoke to her mother about the process and what had been happening. Her mother seemed distracted and agreed with everything she said.

It felt like they were both ready to forget the land when they weren't there. It made her feel bad for her grandparents' legacy—though they'd both known how Sandra felt about the property. Had they thought Sarah might inherit it since she loved the place so much as a child?

She was determined not to feel guilty about the life she'd worked so hard to achieve, even if it wasn't what her grandparents might have hoped would happen. She drove back to the house, wondering what Jack would make of a new buyer popping up so quickly after Leland's death. She looked for him to suddenly appear as she made a few trips in and out of the house with her belongings, but he seemed to be off somewhere else.

Sarah had an idea about a way to say thank you to him by making him dinner. She was good at making one impressive dish—a chicken pot pie that everyone had always raved about. She'd never tried making it in a real oven before, just a microwave. But she thought it would still be good.

She was surprised, and a little worried at first, when Jack wasn't at the house. But she finally convinced herself not to search for him and unpacked everything so she could start making the pot pie. He was bound to turn up at some point.

The chicken and vegetables smelled good while they were cooking but she didn't try to make her own crust as she usually did. She'd bought two crusts from the store and used them. She hoped it would be as good as she put it in the oven to bake.

Sarah took out her laptop while the pot pie was baking, and looked up what she could find about the Blue Way project. It was a huge venture that was linking many trails and other natural sites from the Virginia mountains to the coast. Misty River was a tiny speck on the map for it, but from what she read, Ron was right. It was a big deal for the community. She hoped the next buyer would still want to designate a portion of land on the river for it.

"I guess Nash called with a new buyer." Jack looked over her shoulder.

She didn't jump—she was finally getting used to him popping in and out when she least expected it. "I was looking at the new buyer and the Blue Way. I can't tell from his online profile if he's interested in being part of the project or not."

"You could ask before you sell him the land."

"I will, although I wouldn't refuse to sell it to him if he doesn't want to be part of it."

He squinted at the text she was reading. "Davis Hudson. He's a land developer."

"Probably not interested in the pumpkin patch or the swing by the river." She closed the laptop. "But I knew that was possible."

"You don't have to sell to him either."

"But I have to sell to someone." Sarah got to her feet. "I made dinner if you'd like to eat with me."

He looked surprised. "You cook?"

"You mean a woman can't be a lawyer and a good cook?"

"The thought never crossed my mind." He grinned. "Sure. I'd love to have some of whatever it is that smells so good. Thanks."

"I promise not to talk about what you should do with your life."

"And I promise not to try to influence you to stay."

That made her look up sharply. "I don't know why you'd even think about it. I've never said anything about staying."

"It's not what you've said," he replied quietly. "It's the way you look when you stare out at the fields and the pumpkin patch. Some of that little girl who loved to be here is still inside you."

She laughed as she put on new oven mitts to remove the pot pie. "I'm sure she is, but grown-up me has a job she loves in Richmond where her very nice apartment is and her friends and family live."

Jack took two of the freshly washed china plates out of the dish drainer and put them on the table. "Richmond isn't that far away for family, and you can make new friends."

"I thought you weren't going to try to influence me to stay." She put the hot casserole dish on the pot rest. "Why the sudden hard sell?"

"I didn't know anything about you. Not as an adult. Now I do."

"You've only known me a few days. Just because I love this place doesn't mean I won't sell it."

He put out forks and spoons. "Did you just hear yourself? That's why I think you should stay."

"Not because if I stay you can stay too?"

"Not at all." He held her chair for her. "I'll leave tonight if that will make you stay."

She stared at him over the fragrant chicken pot pie in the center of the table. "You're the strangest man I've ever met. I don't understand why you care so much about this land."

"Everyone needs something they're passionate about. Shall I serve?"

Sarah gave them both a spoonful of pot pie on their plates. Jack poured glasses of sweet tea. They sat opposite each other as they ate.

"Well since you broke your promise not to convince me to stay, I'm going to break mine about not convincing you to think about your future."

"The pot pie is delicious. Your grandmother's recipe?"

"Yes. My mother never cooked anything this difficult in her life."

She spent the next few minutes trying to convince him that he should think about what he'd do next and prepare for the future. He seemed more immune to that than she was to selling the farm.

But after his suggestive words, her mind was buzzing with all sorts of farm activities and reopening the pumpkin patch. She thought about chickens and going out to help her grandmother find the eggs. The farm was beautiful in the spring with the pink dogwoods blooming and new life returning.

"So you'll stay?" he finally asked.

"No, I won't stay. I don't know anything about running a farm."

"I'll teach you." He glanced across at her, his eyes sincere. "Or you can hire someone to work with you."

"You don't know me as well as you think," she debated. "I'm a city girl. The only things I know about keeping this place going are from my memories as a child. That's not much help. I wouldn't even know what to tell someone to do."

"Not a problem then. I'll stay as long as you need me."

"Why?" Sarah pushed her mostly empty plate out of the way.

"Because you care about this place as much as Bess and Tommy did. Because I promised them I'd look after it. They saved my life. I wouldn't have made it through my childhood without them. I think that's worth some time and effort, don't you?"

Chapter Nineteen

She thought about it and shook her head. "It doesn't matter. I'm not staying. I appreciate all you've done, but this isn't my life. I'm sorry."

"I have something to show you." He got up and put their plates in the sink. "Wait five minutes and then come out to the pumpkin patch. Thanks for dinner."

"There's nothing you can show me in the pumpkin patch that will change my mind." She looked back but was talking to an empty kitchen. "Really. I'm not staying."

Sarah ran her gaze over the cabinets and the familiar wall plaques. It felt like her childhood was here instead of in the home her parents had left behind in Suffolk. Jack was right that she loved this place.

But he was wrong thinking she'd stay and bring it back to life. Maybe she could hire him to manage it, as Ron had suggested someone should. It would be worth a shot asking him.

She considered telling him that she'd stay if he'd leave, as he offered to do. Once he was gone, she could sell the place. But that seemed wrong. She didn't want to hurt him. There had to be another way.

After he left, she washed the dishes, silverware, and glasses. It had been at least five minutes. Probably more. She opened the back door and started toward the pumpkin patch.

There was a faint glow coming from it—like the last embers of a fire—or the beginning of one.

"Jack!" she yelled and started running in that direction. She got to the edge of the acres where the pumpkins were growing. He was waiting for her. "What's going on?"

"Look. It's something Tommy did every year when the harvest was over."

Sarah walked out to the field. Jack had carved at least a hundred pumpkins and put candles in them. There were funny faces, scary faces, and pictures of things like bats, cows, and other things she couldn't identify.

"You did all this?" she asked.

He nodded. "I had a few hours free today."

"It's beautiful. Thank you. I was here one weekend when Grampa did this. He wasn't as good an artist as you. I think this is what you should be doing instead of hiding out from everything."

She knew she'd hit a nerve when he turned away. She'd been right about him using the farm as a means of not facing the world. She wanted to ask if he was still getting away from his childhood or if something else had happened to him.

Sarah turned to ask him about it, but as she did, the lights in the house went dark.

"I see it," he said. "Looks like we've got company."

"Treasure hunters?" she whispered, unconsciously moving closer to him.

"Probably not. Stay here. I'll check it out."

"Not on your life. I don't want you to be charged with another murder. You need a witness. And I'm not staying here alone."

"Then stay close and be quiet."

"You don't have to tell me that!"

"You're still talking."

Jack walked slowly toward the house, staying in the shadows. Sarah was right behind him, almost too close since she bumped into him twice when he stopped.

"Sorry," she muttered. "There's someone on the second floor. I think that's a flashlight going through the house."

"Looking for something," he guessed. "I don't suppose you've got your little pistol?"

"No. Sheriff Morgan still has it. But I know where the shovel is."

"Thanks. We'll see if we need that."

She followed him another few steps. "What if it's the killer? He could take us both out. No one would know."

"Then we better see him before he sees us."

They moved stealthily into the house. It was too quiet and creepy knowing someone was upstairs rummaging through her things. What were they looking for? "Maybe we should call the sheriff."

"We will—after we catch this guy."

There were footsteps on the stairs. Sarah looked for something she could use to defend herself and picked up an iron skillet.

"Are you going to hit the bullets back at him?" Jack's voice was slightly below a whisper and close to her ear.

"At least I have something to use against him." She slapped the skillet against her hand and winced. "This thing is heavy."

"I knew I should've locked you in the barn."

"I'm not a kid anymore. I'd just get out."

The footsteps on the stairs slowed and stopped. Sarah panicked as she realized the intruder had probably heard them talking. She held her breath for a moment as she lifted the skillet up to her shoulder ready to battle their attacker.

Jack reached beside him and switched on the kitchen light.

Blinking quickly, Sarah wondered why in the world he'd done such a thing, ruining their element of surprise. Her eyes focused quickly on the man who was still on the stairs.

"Mace?" she gasped, still ready to hit him with the skillet.

Even more of a surprise—Jack was on the stairs with his arm around his throat. When had he moved? He'd been right next to her.

"What are you doing here?" Jack questioned him.

There were only gurgling sounds coming from the realtor.

"Maybe you should let go of him so he can sit down and tell us about it."

Jack grunted and released him. Mace glanced at him before he stumbled down the last few stairs and sat at the kitchen table.

"I'm so sorry," Sarah said. "Do you want some tea?"

"What was he trying to do?" he demanded in a raspy voice. "He could've killed me."

"You were trespassing." Jack followed him to the table. "Why are you here?"

"I was just looking out for Ms. Tucker's interests." He cleared his throat and scooted away from Jack. "I saw the lights on in the house. I didn't want her to have a large power bill. I knew she wasn't staying here."

"Now the truth," Jack encouraged.

"I don't know what you mean," he denied. "I only turned the power off. I was going to lock the doors, and then you came in. I thought you were a treasure hunter."

Sarah didn't know if she believed him either. "Then why were you skulking around in here with a flashlight?"

Mace glanced at Jack. "I thought I heard a noise upstairs. I was checking for rats before I bring the new buyer out tomorrow."

Jack and Sarah exchanged looks across the table.

"It's possible," she said.

"But doubtful," Jack replied.

"Let me make you some hot tea for that throat," she offered.

"I'm sorry," Mace said to both of them. "I didn't realize you were here. I didn't mean to alarm you."

He was shaking all over like a leaf in a winter storm. Sarah could understand his fear after finding himself with Jack choking him.

"Tell us about the new buyer," Jack said.

"G-gladly." The realtor adjusted his glasses and started talking about Davis Hudson as Sarah made tea for him.

She offered Jack a cup too. He refused, and she made one for herself instead.

"I think this is a wonderful opportunity," Mace continued after extolling Mr. Hudson's financial virtues. "H-his offer is almost as good as Leland's but he isn't interested in the Blue Way."

"What does he want with the property?" Jack asked.

"I believe he plans to live here as a gentleman farmer. He was talking about building a new house and raising horses. I don't know if he'll keep the pumpkin patch. But Ms. Tucker didn't make that a deal-breaker."

"No." She sat at the table with her tea. "That sounds fine."

"I probably should be going." Mace eyed Jack suspiciously. "I am free to go, right?"

"Yes. But next time you plan to visit, call ahead." Jack's gaze was steady.

"Oh, I will." He got to his feet on wobbly legs. "Goodnight, Ms. Tucker. Again, I'm sorry for the interruption. I'll see you tomorrow."

Jack said he'd walk him out to his pickup. It wasn't an invitation. Sarah tidied up nervously when they were gone. She heard the truck leave the driveway and waited for Jack to return.

When he didn't come back right away, she found him walking around the outside of the house, apparently looking for something.

"Do you think someone else is out here?" She watched his furtive movements.

"Just being careful."

She followed him as he checked behind all the shrubs. Now was as good a time as any to mention him staying in the house. "You should stay in the house tonight."

He looked back at her in surprise. "I'll check everything before you go to bed. You should be safe."

"That's not what I meant." She started over. "You can't sleep in the barn. There are three bedrooms and a sofa in here. I was surprised that you weren't living in the house anyway. I'm sure my grandparents didn't mean you should take care of the property and live in the barn."

"I never considered living in the house."

"Maybe you should consider it tonight—or until the barn isn't a crime scene."

"I'll be fine."

"You keep saying that, but you don't do anything to make it happen. The spring house is too small and damp to sleep in. The other outbuildings are falling apart. Stay in the house tonight. If it makes you feel better, you can pretend that I'm really scared someone might come in and you're protecting me."

They'd reached the back porch. He looked up at the night sky. "Then I'll sleep out here on the porch."

"I wasn't planning on taking advantage of you or anything," she argued. "You don't have to worry. You'll be safe from me even if you sleep in the house."

He moved closer to her and she tensed, thinking how quickly he'd grabbed poor Mace by the throat.

"What if you're not safe with *me* in the house?"

Sarah considered her response. "I always sleep with a baseball bat under the bed. Something Grampa taught me. I'm not worried about you."

He chuckled. "Goodnight, Sarah."

"Goodnight, Jack."

"Think about what I said about you staying here

permanently."

She opened the kitchen door. "Only if you think about what I said about getting a life."

He muttered something she didn't understand, but she didn't ask him to repeat. She went in the house and closed the door, thinking he was calling her something less than pleasant under his breath.

Sarah turned off the kitchen light and went slowly through the rooms in the old house. She had pleasant memories of each spot. There were potholders she'd made with her grandmother in the kitchen and the lace doilies she'd at least attempted to make in the small living room.

Upstairs, she wandered through the three bedrooms, ending up in her grandparents' room. Here were their lives in old photos—her, Dusty, her mother. There were pictures of her grandparents when they were young and just settling in at the farm. Sarah looked through her grandmother's jewelry box and found dozens of personal items that she couldn't believe her mother had left behind for so many years.

It was the same with her grandfather's top drawer in his clothes chest. Pictures of when he was in the army as a young man were beside bits and pieces of keys, flint, and other things that he'd held dear.

Seeing those things hardened her resolve about finding her grandparents. They didn't voluntarily leave so much of their lives behind.

She sat on the big, lumpy bed and cried. This was why no one thought her family had cared about them. What if Jack hadn't been here and teenagers had broken in and stolen all these things—maybe burned the place down? What had her mother been thinking, leaving everything important here? When she left this time, all of this was going back with her.

Sarah lay back on the bed. Was Jack right about her wanting to stay here? She'd enjoyed the last few days, but it would be different living here all the time. Why had he really thought she would stay? The possibilities of not going back had never crossed her mind before he'd said it. Now it plagued her until she almost couldn't think of anything else.

She closed her eyes but knew she wouldn't sleep, not with all these things buzzing around in her head. "I hope what I said keeps you awake too."

Chapter Twenty

The next morning, Sarah was up early. She'd finally fallen asleep on her grandparents' bed. She hadn't taken the pretty green shawl from her mother's bedroom, but it was thrown across her.

Jack. He wouldn't sleep in the house but didn't mind creeping around after she was asleep.

She looked out on the back porch but didn't see any sign of him. He was probably busy doing whatever he did around the farm. She went back upstairs to shower and dress, putting on her blue suit that didn't look so bad after all.

By the time she was dressed, she smelled bacon, coffee, and either biscuits or pancakes cooking. The mother cat and her kittens were sleeping on the stairs. She almost tripped over them, but they didn't move them out of the way.

Jack put breakfast on the table as she walked into the kitchen. He was freshly showered—there was a shower in the barn. He'd also shaved again and changed into another clean shirt and jeans.

"Good morning," he said. "I thought you'd need something to eat with everything going on today."

There were pancakes on the table beside the bacon and orange juice.

"I didn't buy any bacon when I shopped." She sat at the table.

"Nope. But Gray had plenty. I got it from him. Everyone needs protein."

"I see. Well, thanks. And don't think I didn't notice that you were in here last night."

"I never said I thought you were stupid." He sat opposite her. "I'd like to go into town with you today."

"You need something?"

"I'm more worried that you might need someone."

She poured thick maple syrup on her pancakes. "And you're going to choke anyone who gets in my way? Not a good idea with you being out on bail."

"I already talked to Ben's brother. He knows I might have to knock a few heads together. He's okay with it."

Sarah glanced across at him with one brow raised. "Really?"

"Just kidding." He poured coffee. "Did you think about staying here last night?"

"Not at all."

"You're a terrible liar."

"And you make good pancakes." She met his inquisitive gaze. "Did you think about moving on with your life?"

"Probably not as much as you thought about my suggestion."

"I guess neither of us is going to pay any attention to the other."

"I don't know about that," he replied smoothly. "I think you'll come to your senses."

She laughed. "I feel the same way about you."

He ate a strip of bacon. "What are your plans before you meet the new buyer?"

"I'm planning to visit the county historic museum, and go to the courthouse to get a copy of the deed. My mother can't find her copy, if she ever had one."

"Don't take this the wrong way, but I thought lawyers were better organized."

"Not the ones in my family. Except my father, who had nothing to do with this property, or I'm sure it would've been sold sixteen years ago."

Her phone rang. It was Clare. "Are you ever coming back? What's going on out there?"

Sarah excused herself from the table to talk to her boss. "Right now, I'm not sure when I'll be back. I've been handling most of the work on my laptop. If anything comes up, you can send people to me online. Almost everyone sends information or requests through email now. I shouldn't miss much."

"If you need me to, I can still come down there and strong arm people with my senatorial charm and might," Clare offered with a laugh. "Although you're more likely to wield my charm and might better than I can. If you need to get things moving, don't hesitate to use my name. I'm going to miss playing tennis with you this week. Get everything wrapped up. I need you back here."

"Thanks for being so understanding and supportive. You're the best boss in the world."

"Yes, I am. Let me know if anything shakes loose today. Talk to you later."

Sarah ended the call and put the phone in her handbag. "I'll help you clean up," she said to Jack.

"You barely ate anything."

"I'm completely fortified," she assured him. "That's more than I usually eat in a day."

"That explains it." He set the dishes in the sink.

"Explains what?" She bristled.

"Lack of organization. I'll bet your mother doesn't eat breakfast either."

"I doubt it. She eats less than I do."

"Organization comes from a good breakfast. Ask any general. An army marches on its stomach."

"I'll bear that in mind," she promised. "Leave the dishes. I'll wash them when we get back."

Jack let the mother cat and kittens out of the house before he closed the door.

"Does she have a name?" Sarah asked, taking out her car keys.

"Not that I know of. I found her one night during a storm. She was out in the rain with her babies. I brought her in the barn, and she's hung around ever since."

"You should give her a name. She obviously likes you."

"I can't. Not with my future plans so uncertain. It would be cruel to lead her on that way."

"You're witty today," she remarked as she got behind the wheel. "I guess breakfast is good for organization, but not for common sense, huh?"

Jack didn't comment as she started the car and left the farm.

Score one for me! I left him speechless. She smiled.

"Why are you going to the historic museum?" he asked when they were on the highway.

"Because I'm curious about the gold hunting," she admitted. "I'd like to know if there really is gold hidden on the property. Wouldn't you?"

"And you think they'll know at the museum?"

"I think they'll know if it's historically accurate."

"What then?"

"I don't know. I'll have an interesting party story to tell, I guess."

"You think finding out the truth about the gold could help you find your grandparents."

"Maybe. It's possible something happened to them because of the gold, like Ron said, but not that I think you killed them to find it."

"It would be counterproductive, wouldn't it? If I thought they knew where the gold was and I killed them, I'd never find it."

"Anyway, since we're hiring new private detectives to look for them, I thought this could be a lead."

"Is that what *Ron* said?"

She turned on the street where a brown sign pointed to an old building. "He's a police officer," she reminded him. "He's been trained to look for answers. It can't hurt to try his theories."

"Whatever you say."

Sarah ignored him as she parked and then got out of the car to go inside. Jack went with her, standing close by, his gaze clearly surveilling the area around the museum.

The squat, brown, two-story house had an entrance in the back beside a small parking lot. The houses around it looked old. Huge trees and shrubs grew heavily along the side of the brick walls.

Inside, it was cool and dark. There were dozens of black and white pamphlets near the door. They explained to visitors that the museum was set up to be a self-guided walking tour. One of the areas was designated for the effects of the Civil War on local people and places.

"This could be it," she said. "Maybe there will be some answers here."

"I doubt it." He glanced around without interest.

She went directly to a door marked *Staff* and knocked on it. A small, delicate man in a three-piece suit took one look at her and closed the door again.

Jack laughed quietly. She shot him an angry look.

Sarah knocked again. This time the response was verbal.

"The museum is self-guiding," the man's voice said through the door. "Please choose a tour that interests you."

"I'd like to ask a few questions about the Civil War tour," she told him. "Are you the curator?"

"No. Follow the tour. I can't help you. It's against museum regulations to interact with visitors."

"That's crazy. Please open the door. I have questions that may be a matter of life and death."

The man partially opened the door again and peeked out at her. “What do you want? Maybe I can help you.”

Jack used his finger to push the door open a little farther. “We’d like to see who we’re talking to. If you’re not the curator, who are you?”

“I’m the museum director, Robert Glossom.” He squared his shoulders, looked up at Jack, and gulped. “What is it you need? I can tell you that if you’re here to rob the museum, we have no money on the premises—or anywhere else for that matter. Maybe you should try the convenience store at the corner.”

“We’re not here to rob you,” Sarah assured him. “We’re from Misty River. We’re looking for information about a stash of gold that belonged to the Confederacy. I think I might own the land where the gold was hidden.”

He smiled and shook his head. “People never cease to amaze me. Why does anyone put such stock into old folklore like this?”

“There must be something,” Jack said. “People have been digging for it a long time.”

She was relieved. “Are you saying it’s not real? There wasn’t a trunk of gold buried out there after the Civil War?”

“I’m not saying that…exactly.” He turned to lock his office door. “Come with me. I do know a little something about this.”

They followed him up the stairs to the local Civil War area. There were a few cannons that had nearly rusted to pieces, a few cannon balls, and a mannequin wearing a moth-eaten uniform. Sarah glanced at a diorama of the area which showed the battles and skirmishes around the county.

“Guess they didn’t do much fighting in Misty River.” Jack pointed to the empty space on the map.

“That’s because there was nothing there at the time,” Glossom said tartly. “The Misty River community wasn’t founded for another fifty years after the end of the war. Mostly the battles in this area took place where there were actually people. That area was small, poor farms. They had nothing to gain from the war since they had no slaves or plantations."

"I see." Sarah slid her gaze from the map to the man. "So what can you tell us about the gold?"

"One thing I can tell you—there are tales of unclaimed gold in almost every Confederate state. I believe it was wishful thinking that created them. 'If the armies of the South had just received that last bit of gold, it would've changed the tide of the war.' Blah. Blah. Blah."

"No one knows that for sure," Jack reminded him. "Not even you."

"Maybe not, but the South was doomed from the beginning. They went steadily downhill from there and ended up with a lot of dead soldiers and burned property. They never really even touched the North. Sad but true."

"And the gold?" She tried to put the conversation back on track.

"Yes. Our local chest of gold folklore revolves around three men who were taking the gold to an unknown general when they received word that the South had surrendered. The men decided amongst themselves that this had become a losing proposition and that they would keep the gold."

"And it was buried on a farm in Misty River?" she prodded.

"As I mentioned, there were no soldiers from that area. They wouldn't even have had the money to afford a uniform, which soldiers bought for themselves at that time. Why bury the gold in Misty River if you weren't from there?"

"Why bury the gold at all?" Jack asked. "Why not just spend it?"

"It would have stood out at that time," Glossom replied. "If they'd been able to get it to New York or Boston, it would've been another story. There they could've lived as kings. Northern troops sweeping through this area to quell any remaining rebellion would have taken it from them."

"So you're saying there probably was gold and the three men buried it to use it at a later time," Sarah interpreted. "But not in Misty River."

"It's unlikely. But if something of that nature had happened, the men would have been from the wealthier, western end of the county. They would've buried it on their own land."

"That's good news," she said. "Thank you."

"You mean you aren't trying to find the gold yourself?" the director asked.

"No," Jack replied.

"Like I said." Sarah tried to clarify. "I own the property everyone thinks the gold is buried on."

"You mean the Denning farm." Glossom nodded. "Yes. I know that name. Actually, the odd part about it is that one of the three men who supposedly took the gold was named Denning. Big Mike Denning, who went on to later find a fortune panning for gold in the Misty River. He's well known throughout the county."

Chapter Twenty-One

"Let me get this straight," Jack said with a wry smile. "People believe that Big Mike Denning found gold panning in Misty River, but not that he took Confederate gold?"

Glossom faltered at his words, a troubled look on his face. "It might sound the same, but I assure you it's not."

"The gold is in the river," Jack finished. "Not buried on the property."

Sarah grinned. "So it would seem. Why didn't anyone ever put those things together?"

"Truly," Glossom went on. "It couldn't have happened that way. Gold bullion is much different than gold found in rivers. He would have had to spend years smelting it and breaking it into smaller pieces. It's unlikely."

"He had plenty of time, according to you," Jack added.

"But the probability is very low."

"And I bet I know where it is," Sarah said.

"The marker in the river!" Jack grinned.

"Exactly!"

Glossom seemed upset by their conversation. "There's absolutely no proof of what you're saying. Even if there were, someone would have found it years ago."

"Probably not if they were too busy digging holes in the ground," Sarah said.

"What were the names of the other two men?" Jack asked.

"Let me think." Glossom tapped his head with his finger. "There was Epsom Clapp . . . I think. And the third man—his name is right on the tip of my tongue."

Jack and Sarah waited, but the director couldn't think of the third man's name.

"This is my cell phone number." Sarah wrote her number down for him. "Would you give me a call if you think of it?"

"Sure. It's funny how you can remember something but not quite retrieve it. I'll call you when it comes to me."

"Thanks, Mr. Glossom. You've been very helpful." Sarah shook his hand before she and Jack left the museum.

"Does this mean you're going treasure hunting now?" Jack asked when they were back out in the sunshine.

"No. It means I'm going to get a copy of the deed before I meet with the new buyer."

"You mean knowing there could be gold in the river won't keep you from selling the property?"

"That's what it means." She turned to him. "I agree with Mr. Glossom. Even if there was gold in the river, I'm sure it's long gone. Big Mike probably made sure of that. You've been up and down that stretch—have you ever seen gold in the water?"

"No," he admitted.

"But you think it's there?"

"I don't know. Other people do. It looked to me like Glossom might even come try his hand at it now that he's been enlightened."

Sarah opened the car doors with the key fob. "I wonder

what Grampa would think about all this. I know what my grandmother would say. She only believed in things she knew to be true. I don't think she'd like the idea of people looking for gold."

She started the car, but Jack didn't get in. "Something wrong?"

"I have a few things I need to look into—you're always telling me I should get ready for the future." He smiled. "I'll see you back at the farm. Don't worry. I won't leave without saying goodbye first."

"All right. I'll see you later." She was surprised by that, but maybe it was a good thing. She really didn't need him to squire her around town and end up with her at the real estate office. Sarah considered calling her mother about the new turn of events, but she didn't think her mother would be any more impressed by talk of gold in the river than she was.

Sarah watched him walk away, his hands in the pockets of his jeans, before she pulled out of the parking lot and left the museum.

The courthouse wasn't far. She parked and went inside. There was a long line at the single clerk's window where she had to wait. It seemed to be a good day for making copies of legal documents.

She finally paid her money and received a brand new copy of the deed. There were dozens of names listed above her grandparents' on the document. Not all of them were Dennings. Sarah glanced at the paper and then put it in her pocketbook as her phone rang.

"Hey beautiful." It was Ron. "I'm free for lunch. How about you?"

"I'd like to, but I have a meeting with a new buyer. Maybe later?"

"That works. Looks like you'll be here a while since you can't sell while the land is being used as collateral to keep Jack out of jail. Have you seen him lately, or has he taken off?"

"He didn't do anything wrong. He's still here."

"What is it with that guy? Everyone thinks the world of him, and he's never worked a day in his life."

"I don't know, but I have to go. I'll talk to you later. Thanks for calling."

Sarah put her phone away and started back to Misty River. Mace had left her an email to meet him at the farm when she got back. He'd be out there showing the place to Davis Hudson.

With any luck, this would be it, and Mr. Hudson would sign to purchase the property when it was free of the bail bondsman's claim against it. Naturally, if something happened that the property was forfeit because Jack left, Mr. Hudson wouldn't be the new owner.

But she was sure Jack would honor his pledge to stay until the trial. She thought she could convince Mr. Hudson of that fact too.

What would happen to Jack then?

As far as she knew, he was really only a suspect in Leland's murder. Sheriff Morgan had bowed to the DA's pressure to arrest his best suspect. If the DA brought people from Misty River to testify against him, there would be a lot of words like crazy, squatter, and others less complimentary used against him, but there would also be people who thought the world of him like Gray and Kathy.

The sheriff would no doubt testify to Jack's aggressive behavior against people who were looking for gold on the property. That could make a slam dunk for the prosecution. Jack had no way to defend himself.

Could she carve enough time out of her schedule back home to represent him during a trial? Or would she have to hand him over to a newbie public defender? She wasn't sure how Clare would feel about her attorney taking on a murder case.

She shouldn't feel guilty about what happened. It had nothing to do with her. The closest she could come to a motive for Leland's death was that someone didn't want him to buy the land.

But what about George Burris's death?

Again—someone had probably killed him as a warning not to get rid of the land. The killer liked the way things were, even with Jack out there.

Or maybe the killer was also a treasure hunter who thought he could get rid of Jack at the same time that he scared away potential buyers. In that scenario, Sarah went back to Richmond for another few years and Jack went to prison. The gold hunter had complete access.

Obviously, this alleged person didn't have enough money to buy the land outright. He was relying on what he could do to make it work his way.

Sarah got a call from Kathy as she reached the small green sign on the highway that declared she was in Misty River.

"I told you I'd look into who sells that rifle you found at the murder scene," she said. "Ben and I were at a gun store in Silver Springs. We talked to the man who runs it—Sonny Willis—remember him? He used to have that huge appliance on his mouth to straighten his teeth."

"I don't remember anyone like that. I suppose he came to the pumpkin patch, but I didn't pay any attention."

"Well, anyway, he's grown up real nice now. I was thinking maybe you'd like to go out with him before you leave. Unless you're too busy with Jack. Or Ron." She giggled.

"What about the rifle? Can we talk about that before we discuss my love life?" Sarah asked with a smile. If she was here much longer, she'd be married again.

"Okay. I was getting to that. Sonny said he sold one of those 357 Rugers right before you came back. He said he sold it to Mace Nash. Sonny says Nash has quite a collection of hard-to-find guns. He's always around when things happen. I wonder if he could be the killer."

In a way, it would make sense. Sarah had already signed the paperwork to let Mace take over the land until he sold it. "But why show it to people if he doesn't want to sell it?"

"He's got to make it look good, right? Or you might let someone else sell it. I just wanted to give you a head's up because I know you're meeting with him again. I'm going to have lunch with Ben before we come home. Watch your back."

Sarah thought about the conversation as she drove to the farm.

Killing her wouldn't help Mace with his search for the gold. He'd be in the best possible position to look for it after she went home. She could understand him killing Leland, even though he pretended to make a big show out of wanting the sale.

That could put Davis Hudson's life in jeopardy. Surely the realtor wouldn't think he could get away with blaming three murders on Jack.

She drove quickly down the gravel road to the house hearing the rocks beat against the underside of the rental car. The familiar red pickup was parked in the drive, but there was no sign of either man. Sarah was glad she'd left Jack in town in case Mace had made the mistake of thinking he was out there like usual.

Without hesitating, Sarah called Sheriff Morgan to let him know her suspicions. He told her that he'd get out there as quickly as possible and that she should go up to the Quik-Chek and wait there for him.

"I'm sure there's another explanation for what's going on," the sheriff said. "I've known Nash most of my life. I don't think he's out there shooting people who want to buy your property, Ms. Tucker. But let's not take any chances."

Sarah thanked him and started to back out of the drive when she heard the first shot ring out. It startled her, and she realized the sheriff was right—she needed to get out of there.

Two more shots exploded from somewhere beyond the springhouse. One of them put a hole in the passenger side of her windshield, and the other hit her front tire. The air gasped out, leaving the car lurching to one side. Too late to run now, she got out of the car to hide next to the house. She wasn't sure if she was personally in danger or if Mace was getting rid of another buyer.

A dirty black pickup stopped at the foot of the drive. Jack saluted the driver as he climbed out of the passenger side.

No! This was the worst possible moment he could be back. Another shot rang out. Sarah was worried that Jack could be a target too. As the black pickup drove away, she tackled him, knocking him into the grass.

Chapter Twenty-two

"You can't be here now," she explained quickly as she pinned him. "Keep your head down. I think Mace is killing another buyer."

"I don't think he's killing anyone, Sarah," Jack said. "I appreciate you trying to save my life though."

She put her hand over his mouth. "Quiet. I've already called the sheriff, but he won't be out for a while. If Mace doesn't kill you, he'll try to frame you for this murder too."

He slowly moved her hand. "Why don't we actually find out what's going on? Mace has always been a good man. It's hard to believe he'd kill anyone."

Sarah told him about the rifle purchase. "The police have that gun now, but Sonny says he has others. He brought Davis Hudson out here to kill him like he did Leland so no one would buy the land and he could look for the gold after I'm gone."

Jack put his hand on her forehead. "You feel a little

feverish to me. That's the only reason I can imagine you acting this way. Let's go in the house, and you can lie down with a cold compress on your head. You'll feel a lot better."

Another two shots were fired. The first one hit the side of the house. Someone yelped after the second shot.

"See? I told you. We should hide until the sheriff gets here," she recommended.

"I'll take a look. You go inside. There's a reasonable explanation for this. Believe me, the man who killed George and Leland didn't take random shots before he hit them. He was an expert. This is something else."

"I'm not going in the house—not if you're going to see what's happening. I'm your attorney, and my land is keeping you out of jail. I'm going wherever you're going."

"All right." He helped her to her feet and kept hold of her hand as they started toward the house. "Thanks for thinking you were saving my life, anyway. Or was it just making sure I go to court in one piece?"

"Concentrate," she hissed. "You'll get us both killed. I know you don't think Mace is guilty, but I don't think you are either, and I know I'm not. Someone has already killed two people here. We have to be careful."

He gently squeezed her hand. "All right. Let's be very careful. Keep your head down."

They walked around the side of the house staying close to the overgrown shrubs. There was no sign of anyone and no more gunfire.

"Do you think he heard us and he's escaping along the river to Kathy's property? Maybe we should call her and let her know."

"Can you really imagine him escaping along the river?" Jack asked in a low voice. "He fell in twice when he came out to measure how long your part of the shoreline is before you got here."

"I hope he's not headed toward the Pope house," she whispered.

"I hope not too. Gray might shoot him."

There was a rustling from the poplar trees beside the barn. Sarah picked up a rusted piece of metal—probably some part of an old tractor—and got ready to defend herself.

"Just stand back here a minute," Jack advised as he put both their backs against the barn wall. "Let's make sure you aren't about to attack a deer or a skunk."

But it was two men. Mace, and a man Sarah didn't know, finally walked away from the tree line. She held her breath when she saw that both men were covered in blood. The realtor was limping, and the man next to him was holding his hand over his side.

"Nash." Jack stepped away from the wall. "What the hell are you doing out here? The turkey shoot isn't until November."

"Thank God you're here!" Mace released his hold on the heavyset man beside him. "Mr. Hudson wanted to try hunting out here to get the lay of the land."

"First time with a gun in his hands?" Jack knelt before Mr. Hudson and checked the wound in his side. "How did you manage this?"

"The bullet ricocheted." Mace winced in pain "But he kept on firing, even after he'd shot me in the foot." He looked toward where Sarah was standing. "I'm sorry, Ms. Tucker. But I'm sure this will all work out."

"Not with me buying the place," Hudson wheezed. "I'm probably dying. If not, my wife is going to kill me. She warned me about this. I just wanted to see what it was like."

"Lie down here, Mr. Hudson," Jack said. "I don't think you're going to die, but you've got a bullet in your gut. That's never a good thing. Could someone with a cell phone call for an ambulance?"

Sarah called for an ambulance as Mace slowly sank to the ground, groaning as he cradled his foot. Sheriff Morgan rolled up right after and called out her name when he saw the condition of her car in the driveway. She yelled back to him, and he found them waiting beside the barn.

"What's going on out here now?" he asked in a

disbelieving tone as he took in the injured men. "Please tell me you didn't shoot these two, Jack."

"No. He was with me when it happened." Sarah held her hand on Mace's foot to stop the bleeding.

Between them, Mace Nash and Davis Hudson explained how it had happened. Mr. Hudson apologized for shooting everything except for the duck he thought he'd seen in the trees by the river. He started crying when he apologized for shooting Sarah's car and the house.

"I didn't mean to hurt anyone. I'm never picking up another gun."

"Maybe you just need a course in gun safety, my friend," the sheriff said. "I'll call a tow truck for your car, Ms. Tucker."

"Then I won't have any transportation," she complained. "I can call the rental company. They'll take care of it and bring me another car."

"Suit yourself. The car will have to be towed to our impound lot anyway since it's part of a crime."

"A crime?" Davis scrubbed his eyes with his hands and looked up at the sheriff. "I didn't mean for any of this to happen. Do I have to be charged for it?"

"Now that I'm here you do." Sheriff Morgan nodded. "Don't worry. It's a misdemeanor. You won't go to jail unless they want to file more serious charges against you."

"Not me," Mace said. "I still want to sell you this land for your new house and horse stable. We can forget about what happened today."

"I feel the same way," Sarah told him. "As long as you pay for the damages."

"You don't even have to pay for my foot. I'll tell them it happened while I was cleaning my gun."

Jack smiled and turned away.

The ambulance finally arrived as Mace desperately tried to convince Davis that he still wanted the property despite what had happened. Davis was just eager to get on the stretcher and go to the hospital.

"I think you lost this sale," Jack said.

"Yeah. Me too." Sarah stared at the smile curved across his mouth. "You're enjoying this, aren't you? Another buyer bites the dust."

"It happens."

"Never mind. Help me look for where he shot the house, and I'll call the insurance company—I hope we still have insurance"

"Sure. I know where it hit." He led her to a piece of chipped siding before taking out his knife and removing the bullet. "We're lucky he didn't have a Ruger. With his aim, he would've done a lot more damage."

"But I guess we don't like Mace for Leland and George's deaths after all." She looked at the bullet he'd put in her hand.

"Liked?"

"You know." She shrugged. "Like they say on TV."

"It's been a long time since I watched TV."

Sheriff Morgan found them there. "I guess Mace isn't the killer huh, Ms. Tucker?"

"I don't know if this answers that question. I don't think he was trying to kill Mr. Hudson, but he still bought the same gun that you confiscated."

"Don't worry." The sheriff dangled a set of keys in his hand. "Mace told me where his Ruger is. I'm going to take a look at it now. But we know the one we have killed George and Leland. Nobody said he bought two rifles, did they?"

"No," she admitted. "I guess they didn't."

"Leave the investigating to the professionals, please," he said. "I know you're sitting around here with time on your hands because you don't want to leave until this is resolved, but don't put yourself in any further danger."

"From what I understand, you don't have to stay because of me," Jack said. "You can hire an attorney to take care of it so you can go back to Richmond until we find the real killer or I go to trial."

Sheriff Morgan chuckled. "See? There you go. You can

pack up and head out."

"Thanks. I'll check on that." Sarah already knew she didn't have to stay. Anyone could handle the bond issue. But she felt bound to it—and wanted to know what was going on. It wasn't easy to just walk away from what she'd experienced.

Kathy pulled up as the sheriff was leaving. "I heard something was going on over here. Sorry I couldn't get away sooner. Is everyone okay?"

Sarah glanced at Jack before she went down to talk to her friend. When she looked back, he was gone, along with Sheriff Morgan. She filled Kathy in on Mace bringing Davis out to try his hand at hunting. The ambulances were testimony to her story as they left with the two men.

"You've had a busy day. I see Jack is in the wind again. Why don't you come over to my place for a while?"

"I don't know," Sarah hedged. "I should probably wait for them to get my car."

"You don't have to be here for that. If they need you, I'm sure they have your cell phone number. Come on. I promise you a good time and a great meal."

"Okay. Just let me change clothes. I have a feeling whatever your idea is of a good time doesn't involve me wearing this suit or pumps. I'll be right back."

The cell phone rang as Sarah was changing. She'd thought it was the rental car company, but instead it was Ron.

"I just heard," he said. "Are you all right?"

"I'm fine. My car isn't so good, but they're going to bring me a new one." She briefly went through Davis's shooting spree. "I'm on my way over to Kathy's place for a while. I'm hoping everything calms down while I'm gone."

"Did you get that deed for Nash while you were in town?"

"Sure. Not a problem. I also paid a visit to the historical museum. Apparently there really was a chest of gold, but the director doesn't believe it's buried out here. Jack and I had an idea about it being in the river. That would be ironic since everyone wants to dig for it."

"Do you plan to try to find it before you go home?"

"I doubt it, although Jack disappeared again. He might be out there now."

"I'm glad you can still laugh about it. Some people take treasure hunting pretty serious."

"I guess I'm not one of them." Kathy honked her horn. "I should go. I'll talk to you later."

She hung up and finished dressing, putting on her jeans and the old sandals. She couldn't wait to tell her mother how much she'd enjoyed wearing her old clothes. She'd probably be horrified.

With a smile on her face, Sarah skipped downstairs. She half expected to see Jack appear in the kitchen before she left. She was getting too used to seeing him around all the time.

Kathy looked like she was getting ready to honk the horn again when Sarah finally came down the drive. "I was wondering what was taking you so long. Let's get out of here before something else weird happens."

Sarah got in, and they took off. "So, what kind of fun thing are we doing?"

"Ever make apple cider?"

Chapter Twenty-three

Sarah learned more about making apple cider than she'd ever wanted to know. She wasn't overly fond of cider anyway. After peeling and cutting hundreds of apples, she was pretty sure she never wanted to drink it or eat an apple again.

The company was congenial. They worked with Kathy's aunt, Cindy. Ben couldn't be there because he was busy with some other work on the farm. Two neighboring high school girls helped.

The conversation went through every subject. Cindy had been at the barn-raising, too, and mentioned how good Jack looked without his beard and with a decent change of clothes. The two young girls snickered as Cindy wondered if Jack could be domesticated.

Kathy shook her head. "That man won't ever be living happy-ever-after under someone's roof—not for long anyway. That kind never is."

"He's really old anyway," Sheena, one of the high school girls, said. "You should go after someone like Ben. He's hot and not too old."

"Excuse me," Kathy said. "My aunt can't go after my man."

Cindy laughed. "Oh, he's yours now, huh? I saw him with Alice Spencer one day last week at the Burger Shack. They were both real cozy on the same side of the booth—if you know what I mean."

"I'm not worried about Alice Spencer. She's like a friend he grew up with." Kathy brought out another bushel of apples. Everyone groaned.

"When do we get to the fun part?" Sarah asked. "My hands feel like dried apples."

"What kind of things do you do for fun in Richmond?" Cindy asked.

"We go to plays and museums. Sometimes we drive to DC and catch an art exhibit. City stuff, I guess." Sarah smiled when she saw the expressions on their faces.

"Speaking of fun," Sheena said. "The maze just opened yesterday. I haven't gone through it yet this year, but it was a lot of fun last year."

"Especially after dark." Cindy smiled slyly. Both teenagers laughed.

"What kind of maze is it?" Sarah asked.

"It's a corn maze," Kathy explained. "They cut a pattern into the corn, and you have to find your way out. I got lost twice last year."

"Don't they want to sell the corn?" Sarah questioned.

"They're selling it to make ethanol," Cindy said. "It doesn't matter what kind of shape it's in."

"That must be nice," Kathy replied. "Usually, like these apples, everything has a good date. That's why we have to make the last of them into cider."

"What about those pumpkins of yours?" Cindy asked Sarah. "Are you selling those?"

"I haven't really thought about it."

"It's not only about the pumpkins. People use them for pies and pumpkin butter too," Cindy told her. "Not to mention pumpkin bread and roasted seeds."

"I thought it looked like you had a good harvest from the pumpkins I saw at the barn-raising. That's why I asked." Cindy started in on another apple. "I mean, I won't deny that everyone has sneaked into the pumpkin patch down through the years. But you can only carry out so many that way. If we could get your permission before you go, we could come in with trucks and haul them away."

Sarah thought about it. Even though Jack said the pumpkins reseeded themselves, it wasn't necessary to have all of them do it. "Sure. I don't see why not. They're just dying out there."

"Great!" Kathy said. "Thanks. We'll come down tomorrow."

Ben came in with a young man who was a part-time farm worker. He started the apple press to squeeze out the cider. Kathy explained to Sarah that the difference between apple juice and apple cider was that the juice was clarified. No bits of apple.

They gave Sarah the first taste. She was reluctant to drink it and surprised when she enjoyed it. "This tastes amazing. Much different than the kind you buy in the store."

"No wonder," Cindy said. "Everything tastes better when it's fresh. It's one of the perks of living on a farm."

"Whatever you say," Sheena said. "As soon as I finish school, I'm gone. I don't care how fresh the food is. I just want to live in the city with all the conveniences."

"You'll come back," Cindy added. "People always do."

Kathy didn't agree with that. "Kids leave and don't come back. I'm sorry." She smiled at Sarah. "Not like your grandparents. I mean people sell their farms that have been in their families for generations. That's why this area never grows. Kids graduate from high school, and they look for an easier life."

"Yeah." Sheena's heavily made-up eyes returned to

Sarah. "That's right. You're from the ghost house. Are you living there?"

"For a few days," Sarah replied. "But there aren't any ghosts."

"What do you think happened to those old folks who lived there?" Sheena continued, despite warning frowns from Kathy and Cindy. "Some people say it was aliens and they were abducted. Their bodies were probably dropped off in space."

"That's enough of that." Cindy got a few more apples. "I remember Tommy and Bess. Something happened to them, but it wasn't aliens."

"What do you think it was if it wasn't aliens or ghosts?" Sheena asked.

"I think we should talk about something else." Kathy nodded at Sarah. "You didn't know them, and it's a painful memory for other people."

Sheena apologized. "Sorry. I wasn't thinking about it that way. I guess it's been so long. It doesn't seem like anybody would still be alive who knew them."

Cindy laughed at that. "You are such a baby. You'd better get some life experience before you go to the city or those people will eat you alive."

The conversation topic changed as they continued loading the apples into the presser. At the other end, gallons of cider were filled and closed. Kathy, Cindy, and their helpers sealed the tops.

Sarah was exhausted by the time they were finished, but it made her feel good seeing the glass gallons of cider at the side of the kitchen. Making something like this was different than the work she normally did—not that she wasn't proud of the work she did for Clare—it was just unusual to get her hands dirty doing it.

They all pitched in to make supper. Bits of leftover apple were made into fritters that went along with ham and beans. There were leftover biscuits from breakfast that morning and a new wedge of cheese. Kathy had been trying her hand at cheese-making during the year.

But Sheena and her friend left before they could eat. They were on their way to meet other kids at the Burger Shack. She apologized again to Sarah for not considering her feelings about her missing grandparents.

"They're good kids," Kathy said when the girls were gone. "They get caught up in too much other stuff that they don't need in their lives."

Cindy laughed as they set the table. "You were exactly the same way. Your mother was so sure you were going to live your life as a street junkie—she didn't even want you to take an aspirin! Sheena will be fine too. You'll see. She was raised right, with strong roots. You can't beat that."

Ron showed up at the door just as they sat down to eat. Kathy didn't say a word, just made room at the table while Ben got a plate for him.

"What's been going on with that murder investigation?" Cindy asked with no preamble.

"You know I can't talk about all that." Ron smiled at Sarah beside him at the table. "But we're working on it. A few new things have come to light. It's just a matter of time."

Sarah wasn't surprised at Kathy's quick table arrangements that put him beside her. Again, his hand kept wandering across her knee. It seemed rude to mention something that probably shouldn't have bothered her.

"What about Jack?" Ben asked. "Is he still gonna go to jail for the murders?"

"Because we all know there's no way he was responsible," Cindy added. "I've never known a nicer, more respectful man in my life."

"That's because you've never gone over to dig for gold," Ben's young helper declared. "He's like a demon if he doesn't want you there. Half the kids at school are terrified of him."

Ben slapped the back of his head. "I told you not to go over there."

"Sorry." He shrugged. "Everybody does it. You play the

lottery. It's the same thing."

"Trespassing and digging holes in someone else's property is not the same thing as the lottery," Cindy told him. "I keep hearing that the new generation has it all figured out. But they sound as stupid as we ever did."

The boy held his head down but continued eating.

"Let's talk about something else—like Christmas." Cindy smiled. "Now that's a pleasant thought."

The conversation turned to local tree farms and who had the best trees. Kathy talked about wishing she had more land so she could grow grapes for wine as well as fir trees.

"Sounds like Sarah's place is still for sale," Ben said. "We talked about buying her property."

"That's a great idea," Sarah said. "Ron suggested that I leave a manager here if I couldn't sell it. Why don't you two just plant whatever you want? I'll leave something legal in case Mace can sell it. But in the meantime, it would be extra space for you."

Ben and Kathy exchanged interested glances across the table.

"That sounds like it could work," she said. "I'd need some kind of warning time so I could harvest whatever I'd planted."

"Not fir trees," Ben said. "But maybe we could move some of the short term crops over there and you could plant some trees here."

"You don't have to decide tonight," Sarah said. "Think about it. We can talk tomorrow."

"That would give Jack a home too," Cindy said. "I've been worried what would happen to him if the land was sold."

"That way no matter if he worked for me or not, he'd be on my land," Kathy said. "Maybe I could still convince him that I'd be a good boss."

It seemed like a reasonable solution.

Sarah thought Ron would be pleased that she'd taken his suggestion, but he was staring across the kitchen with a scowl on his face. Her cell phone rang before she had a chance to ask him what was wrong. She excused herself and went to answer it on the back porch.

"Is this Sarah Tucker?"

"Yes. Who's this?"

"This is Robert Glossom from over at the historical museum in town. You had a question about the three men that might have taken the Confederate gold."

"Oh. Yes."

"Mind you, I still don't believe that gold is buried on your property—or in Misty River—this is for the sake of argument and historic fact."

"That's fine." She smiled at the qualifier.

"The three men were big Mike Denning, Edward Broadwell, and Barton Clapp."

Sarah gulped and her hands started shaking. She sat on one of the old rocking chairs. There was a dim porch light above her. "Thank you, Mr. Glossom. I appreciate your research."

"Think nothing of it. Thank you for visiting the museum."

She felt a little sick to her stomach after she'd put away her phone. Why hadn't Ron mentioned that their ancestors were in cahoots on the gold? He probably knew. It wasn't like they hadn't talked about the history behind it.

There was this terrible feeling that something was very wrong. But just because one of Ron's relatives was involved with stealing the gold, or whatever happened to it, didn't mean anything today. Her relative was part of it too.

Ron was a deputy—respected in the community. Why was she even thinking that he could be part of George and Leland's murders?

It was crazy, but she couldn't shake the feeling that she'd just learned something important.

Sarah went back to the kitchen. Everyone was clearing the table. She thought about telling them what the research had brought up, but one look at Ron changed her mind.

"Is everything okay?" he asked, coming to her side.

"Yes. Mace has another buyer who's interested in the land." She smiled. "I'm going to talk to him tomorrow."

"Good news," Ron agreed, putting his arm around her and giving her a quick squeeze.

"Darn!" Kathy added. "Just as I was starting to consider the possibilities of using your land. That's not fair."

As Ben promised Kathy that they'd find an alternative to planting short-term crops on the acreage next door, Sarah excused herself, taking her handbag with her to the bathroom. She turned on the light and took out the deed to her land. With her heart beating fast, she read through the list of previous owners.

Close to the top was Edward Broadwell. The land had changed hands quickly—in less than a year Mike Denning was listed as the new owner.

Could that be it? She stared at her pale face in the bathroom mirror. Did Ron feel that he owned the land and the gold? Did he really believe the gold was still on the property?

Kathy's curt knock on the door made her jump. "You okay in there?"

"Yeah. Fine. Thanks."

What should she do now? She'd already jumped the gun telling the sheriff that she thought Mace had killed the two men. She couldn't tell him that she suddenly had a weird idea that his deputy had done it. He'd think she really was insane.

Kathy suggested board games, but Sarah was exhausted again. She could understand why people went to bed early when they got up at dawn—around six p.m. she was already tired.

Besides, she was anxious to tell Jack about her thoughts. She hoped he'd take it seriously.

"I'd like to, but I'd probably fall asleep," Sarah said with a yawn. "I'll be glad to get back to easier work and later mornings."

"When are you going?" Ben asked.

"I'm not sure yet, but I'm going to leave Kathy as the steward of my property." She glanced at Ron, wanting him to know that he wouldn't have free rein with it. "There's the issue with using the land as collateral for Jack's bond, but I'm sure that will pass."

"Or we'll track him down," Ben promised.

Kathy nudged him with her elbow. "Of course Jack's not going to run. He might look like a wild mountain man most of the time, but he has integrity. He knows what he's doing."

Ben offered to take Sarah home—she still hadn't heard from the rental car company.

"I have to leave anyway," Ron quickly volunteered. "I'll be glad to see her home."

Sarah wanted to insist that she go home with Ben, but that could tip Ron off about what she was thinking. If he was guilty of killing the two men, she didn't want him to get away. She had to stay cool and calm, thanking Ron with a polite smile.

After saying goodnight all around, Sarah went out to Ron's car. She tried to keep the conversation light, probably laughing too much and worrying if he would get suspicious. He pulled into the drive and she took a deep breath.

Just let me get out of here and find Jack.

"I'm glad you were able to get the deed for the property today." Ron turned to her.

It was dark and hard to see his face once the car's interior lights were off.

"Yes. And thanks for the idea of finding a manager for it. I feel much better knowing I can leave Kathy in charge. That was such a good suggestion."

"Glad I could help." He reached under his seat and pulled out a large handgun. "Now where's Jack? Out looking for my gold?"

Chapter Twenty-Four

"What's that for?" Her heart thudded in her chest. *Cool and calm*. She tried to take a deep breath but it wouldn't come.

"Let's go inside, Sarah."

"I don't understand." She tried to bluff. "What's wrong?"

"Come off it. I know you went to the museum today, and you got the deed. You've put two and two together by now. That's fine. I'm done playing games. I know you and Jack have been looking for the gold. Don't bother denying it."

"Ron, I—"

"Once I frame Jack for your murder too, he'll be gone for a real long time. Kathy and Ben won't think anything of me coming around to help out. Once I get the gold maybe I'll buy this land—even though by right it should already belong to me. You see, Big Mike killed my great-great uncle, Edward, and took the land and gold for himself."

"Look, you don't have to do this," she said. "It's all ancient history. You can find the gold and take it for all I care. How much do you think is left after people have been searching for two hundred years?"

"We'll see, won't we?" He nudged her with the gun. "Out of the car."

Sarah felt like she had to comply. He got out right behind her, sliding across the seat, and pushed the gun in her side.

"You know, I really like you," Ron said, touching her hair. "You're pretty and smart. I've tried to think of ways to get rid of you without actually hurting you, but you're still here, still in my way."

"I'm not in your way at all," she disagreed. "I just told you that you can have the gold. I don't want it."

"Sure you don't." He sneered. "You want it just like George and Leland did."

Trying to distract him, she went after his actions. "I don't understand why you killed George. I'm guessing Leland was also in your way because he wanted to buy the land."

"George would've told you everything if he'd lived. He was Barton Clapp's great-grandson—Big Mike killed him too. Our ancestors were supposed to share the property so they could split the gold they'd buried here."

"That was a long time ago. But I'm willing to honor that partnership." She had her cell phone in her pocket and was trying to manipulate it so she could call 911. It wasn't easy to do inconspicuously.

"Too late to make new deals, Sarah." He pushed the gun into her ribs. "Start walking."

She walked toward the house, thinking that this would be an awesome time for Jack to do one of his popping up tricks. She might still get shot since the gun was slammed into her side, but she'd have a better chance of survival than she had otherwise.

"It won't do any good to kill me," she argued. "The deed

will just go to my mother and brother. They'll come to see what happened and figure out everything I did."

"I thought about that when I killed George. I meant to kill you, too, but Jack was out here playing the hero as usual. I was glad he did after I'd thought about it. Don't worry. I have a better answer to your death now."

He kept pushing her toward the house. Sarah kept talking, hoping Jack would hear them. Of course this would be the time he wasn't out looking for treasure hunters. He was probably too busy hunting in the river for the gold himself.

"Kathy and Ben know you took me home," she argued. "I think they'll figure it out if I'm dead tomorrow morning. I don't know what your plan is, but it won't work."

"Shut up and get in the house." He pushed her up the front steps and opened the door. "Don't worry. You have company."

"Jack?" she asked with a catch in her voice. That was why he wasn't here. Ron had already taken care of him.

He laughed as he switched on the living room light. "Not this time. But he's gonna be sorry he missed the party. Even Sheriff Morgan is going to believe that he killed you."

"Mace?" Sarah saw the real estate agent and went quickly to his side. He was unconscious on the floor. He'd obviously made it to the hospital to have his foot treated. There was a bandage on it that was tinged with some blood. "Why did you bring him here?"

"Because he's my solution," Ron said. "First he witnesses you signing the deed over to me, its rightful owner. He's a notary, so he can make that transaction official. The sheriff will think Jack was so enraged when he saw you give me the property that he killed you and poor Nash. I was lucky to have survived his rampage with only a few minor wounds."

"I guess you've thought of everything." She moved away from Mace. If Ron wanted him conscious, he could do it himself. "But you know Jack is your wild card, right?"

"I'll take care of Jack. Everyone will know I had to defend myself with lethal force to stop him."

"Too bad you have no idea where he is or when he'll show up," she taunted him. "That must make you kind of nervous."

He glanced uneasily across his shoulder at the living room window and moved to the right of it. "He'll show up. I'll be ready for him. Get Nash on his feet. Let's get this going."

Sarah tried to think of something else to say. She moved slowly toward the unconscious realtor, wondering what she could do to keep this from happening in case Jack didn't show up. There had to be something she could use as a weapon.

Despite not wanting to help him, she had to stall for time. She leaned over Mace and called his name. He didn't stir. "I think I need some water."

"Fine. We'll both go in the kitchen. Don't get any stupid ideas. It doesn't matter to me what order everyone dies in. You could be first."

"I guess you hadn't figured this out yet when you killed Leland and tried to make it look like Jack did it." She walked in front of him toward the kitchen and switched on the light.

"You're right. I thought you'd go away and I could get Jack to take the blame for the two deaths. It would make sense why he'd done it. And what do you mean, trying to make it look like it? Even the sheriff half believes Jack killed those two because he doesn't want you to sell the land."

It was unnerving knowing he'd been thinking this through since she'd met him. It was worse with him standing right behind her preparing to execute his plan. She wished Jack would sneak up on him. But he could be killed, too, if he showed his face. Maybe there was some way she could warn him.

Before she could think of that way, the lights in the house went off. The water had started to trickle out of the faucet, but with the power off, the pump couldn't come on either. The cloth she was holding was barely damp.

"Jack!" Ron pushed the gun into her back. "Mess with me, and she loses a kidney."

There was no response.

"Get back in the living room and wake Nash." He shoved her in that direction.

But when they got in the other room, the realtor was gone. Ron made her sit in one of the chairs while he used a flashlight to search behind the furniture in case his prisoner had crawled away.

Sarah could hear him getting angrier from his heavy breathing and frequent curses. She realized, as he probably did too, that Jack had taken Mace out of the house while they were in the kitchen.

"This doesn't matter," Ron yelled in frustration. "I still have the girl. I can kill her and then look for you and Nash. Remember how I killed George? I don't have the Ruger anymore, but it won't take a rifle to kill Sarah. It'll be like killing Leland and leading you into the trap in the barn. I could've killed you then, Jack. I'll do it tonight and make up for that mistake."

He was whirling around the living room, glaring at the ceiling as though Jack was up there watching him. Sarah realized that she wouldn't get a better opportunity to escape before he made good on his threats.

She slithered off the chair to the floor and crawled around the back of the sofa. Ron was still yelling crazy threats at Jack. She kept crawling until her knees told her that she was in the kitchen. It would only take him a minute to realize she was gone once he stopped ranting. She had to make sure she was in a safe place by then.

Which way would he think she'd go? She could reach the back door and run outside in the darkness of the yard. It would be hard to find her there. But wouldn't he expect her to do that?

She could crawl up the stairs and hide in one of the bedrooms. That seemed like the least expected action, but it might be easier for him to find her.

The choice was made for her when Ron stopped yelling and realized she wasn't in the living room. He swore and ran for the back door, throwing it wide open as he started screaming her name while he hunted for her.

Sarah ran up the stairs, heart pounding. She gulped for breath as she hid in her grandparents' bedroom.

Ron would never be able to search everywhere outside, especially not in the dark. On the other hand, there weren't enough places in the bedroom to hide if he decided to come looking for her here.

She listened but didn't hear anything. Finally realizing she could call for help even if it took a while to get there, she reached for her cell phone.

It was gone. She'd dropped it somewhere, maybe in the house. She'd had it, trying to call without looking as she'd walked inside. It had to be in the living room or coming up the stairs.

She didn't hear any footsteps or heavy breathing—Ron must still be outside. She crept back downstairs, carefully running her hand along the wood, searching for her phone.

No one was *ever* going to convince her that she didn't need a gun for protection. In fact, she planned to buy another one if she survived this.

Sarah was on her knees in the area between the kitchen and the living room when she heard footsteps coming from the back porch. She pushed herself flat against the wall.

"Are you in here?" Ron whispered. "Jack? Where are you? Did you take Sarah too? You can't play these little games with me the way you do with the kids. I've got specialized training that you've never dreamed about."

He brushed by the table, and she went quickly to the other side. But she didn't move fast enough. He reached out and grabbed her hair as she inched by.

She yelled as his rough hold brought tears to her eyes. Her hand banged against the stove. The heavy, cast iron frying pan was still there. He was close to her. With a quick movement, she grabbed the frying pan and hit him as hard as she could.

He didn't release her, but he drew in a short, painful breath and swore at her. She knew she'd hurt him and tried again.

This time, he let her go, moaning and dropping to the floor. She stood over him with the frying pan in both hands ready to hit him again.

"I think you got him," Jack said near her ear. "You win. Let me get the lights."

Sarah wanted to run after him. She wanted to be anywhere except where the man who wanted to kill her was. Her legs wouldn't move. Her head felt like she'd been the one hit with a frying pan. Her knees gave out, and she sank to the wood floor.

The lights came on. Ron was alive but out cold near her feet with a deep, red gash on his head.

"Are you okay?" Jack found her staring at the other man. She didn't reply, even when he took the frying pan away from her and helped her to her feet. "Sarah?"

With a small cry, she threw her arms around his neck and hugged him tightly.

"It's okay," he assured her. "You're fine. And you took care of your boyfriend."

Sarah moved away from him. "Where were you? I don't get one moment's peace around here with you popping up everywhere. Where were you tonight?"

He started to speak.

"And don't you dare tell me you were out looking for that stupid gold in the river. I'll hit you with the frying pan too."

"I was having a drink with Gray and Mary. There was a lot to tell them about the gold and what the museum director said. I started home and saw the light on in the house. Ron was waving the gun around in front of the window. The rest is history. I can guess what his plan was."

"Oh." She sat at the table. "I need a drink." She watched

as Jack tied Ron's hands and feet. "Where's Mace?"

"I would've been back for you sooner, but he woke up as I was moving him and started crying and clinging like a monkey. I couldn't get him to stop. I had to knock him out again and leave him in the barn. I guess I was too impatient with him. You were already taking care of the situation. "

Sarah heard the distant sound of sirens coming toward them. Jack poured her a drink from a jug made of brown pottery. "Tommy made this. It should do the trick."

The rest of the night was a blur after she'd imbibed whatever was in the jug. Sheriff Morgan came and went. She was sure she saw other deputies and paramedics, but she didn't regain full consciousness until the next morning.

"Oh God." She groaned and put her hands to her head. "How much of that stuff did I drink?" Her whole body hurt and her head felt as though it was going to fall off.

"More than I've ever had." Jack was sitting in a chair by the foot of her mother's bed. "You've got quite a tolerance."

"Why didn't you stop me?" She tried to get up, but it hurt too much to move.

"I was afraid you might hit me with the frying pan."

She opened one eye to glare at him. He sounded much too happy. "What's so funny?" Her voice was raspy and thick.

"You—in that bed. Your feet hang off the end. I moved your things into your grandparents' room. At least that way the bed is big enough for you."

"Are we still pretending that I'm going to stay?"

"I've never pretended you were going to stay. The first time I saw you get out of the car, I *knew* you were staying."

Sarah started to argue with him, but that was it. The abuse she'd heaped on her stomach turned on her, and she barely made it to the bathroom.

"That's another plus to your grandparents' room," he said as she sped by. "The bathroom is closer."

Epilogue

Sarah sat on one of the large rocks in the river beside the stone pillar that pointed out the boundaries between counties. The sun was warm on her head even though the water was freezing where her feet rested.

It had been an eventful few weeks since Ron had confessed to killing George Burris and Leland Drake. Her mother had called it a nightmare and offered to come get her. But the worst was yet to happen, at least in her mother's point of view.

Explaining to her parents and her brother that she wasn't going to sell the farm and that she was staying in Misty River was something she wished she could forget.

There had been crying and recriminations. Her father had threatened to cut her out of his will. Her brother had said he'd take her to court for his portion of the land. He'd actually come to the farm but had left quickly when he'd seen the new bee colony that Kathy was helping her start.

Everyone would get over it. She'd been worried about work, but her boss had come through again. Clare still wanted her to work for her, with the occasional trip to Richmond or when she traveled. Sarah would be able to do most of what was needed from her laptop right there in Misty River.

Everyone else seemed unsurprised that she'd decided to stay. Kathy and the Popes had welcome home parties for her. Her life was taking on a new dimension as she and her property manager, Jack Collins, came up with ideas that could make the farm profitable again.

Peggy Lee's husband, Steve Newsome, had called from his office in Charlotte to let her know that he might have found a lead about where her grandparents had disappeared.

"I don't have anything official about this yet, but I thought you'd want to know what I'd found."

"Anything." She put the phone on speaker so Jack could hear too.

"It's possible—and I use that word carefully—that your grandparents were relocated for their safety."

"What?" she asked. "You mean like witness protection?"

"Yes. But it was a long time ago, and information on the program is sketchy. I can't swear you'll ever know for sure. I'm going to send you what I can that made me begin searching in that direction. Keep it to yourself. Don't even share with your local law enforcement. If they were relocated, and are still safe, their lives could depend on it."

Sarah was surprised and happy. "Maybe there's an answer besides ghosts and aliens. Thank you, Steve."

"Sure. And Peggy says you should come visit for Christmas. Her new tree is decorated. We're having a party on the seventeenth. Nothing formal. Come if you can. You can stay with us."

"I'll try to be there." They exchanged goodbyes. Sarah stared straight ahead at the kitchen wall for a long time. "Do you think it's possible?"

"Anything is possible," Jack replied. "Maybe we'll see

them again."

Which had brought them to the river on the last day of November when other people were frantically traveling for the Thanksgiving holiday.

Jack came up out of the water. He was wearing a snorkel and a wet suit against the cold current. In his gloved hand were three pea-sized pieces of gold.

Sarah held out the bowl. "It looks like Big Mike did a good job of hiding the gold."

"I think he spent most of it." Jack looked at the paltry findings in the bowl. "You'll probably make more money on tourists coming to put their kayaks in the river as part of the Blue Way."

She sighed. "Every little bit helps. Is that it for today?"

"I think so. I can't feel my fingers anymore."

"I expected more from you. You seemed tougher."

"Thanks." He pushed himself up on the rock beside her. "You know I get half of this as a finder's fee since I'm always the one in the water."

"You'll have to get in line behind my brother if you want to sue me." She stood up and reached down for the bowl. But before she could get it, he pushed her into the freezing water.

Sarah came up shivering and calling him every name she could think of. "Why did you do that?"

"I just wanted you to have the feeling that you'd done something to earn your share." Jack picked up the bowl and started toward the river bank.

"Hey wait! Aren't you going to help me out? Jack?" she yelled after him. "You can't just leave me here."

"See you back at the house."

From the Pumpkin Patch

Pumpkin Word Lore

Pumpkins date back for hundreds of years. The word 'pumpkin' originated from the Greek word for large melon, pepon. Pepon was changed by the French into pompon. Down through the years, the English changed pompon to pumpion which it remained until the 1700s when the Americans changed it to pumpkin. It has resided there happily ever since.

The pumpkin has been useful to writers almost since it was first named. Shakespeare spoke of 'pumpion' in his *Merry Wives of Windsor* tale. It is also used in *The Legend of Sleepy Hollow, Peter, Peter, Pumpkin Eater*, and *Cinderella*.

Types of Pumpkins

There are dozens of types of pumpkins with many interesting names including Cinderella, One Too Many, and Red Warty Thing. Each has its own colors, sizes, and desirable traits. Choose your pumpkin according to your needs.

- Jack Be Little is a miniature pumpkin variety, perfect for table decoration.
- Autumn Gold is great for carving and decorating. It's a good choice for Jack-o-Lanterns.
- Sugar Treat is just right for cooking and baking.
- Dill's Atlantic Giant variety can grow to 200 pounds. This is a massive pumpkin.

Recipes

Pumpkin Pound Cake

Ingredients:

2 1/2 cups cake flour
1 1/2 teaspoons baking powder
1/2 teaspoon salt
1/2 teaspoon ground ginger
1/2 teaspoon ground nutmeg
1 1/2 teaspoons ground cinnamon
1/2 teaspoon ground cardamom
4 eggs, separated
1/2 teaspoon cream of tartar
1 cup unsalted butter, softened
2 teaspoons vanilla extract
2 cups lightly packed dark brown sugar
1 cup unsweetened pumpkin puree, canned or fresh
Confectioner's sugar (if you'd like to dust the top)

Instructions:

Preheat oven to 350°F and use vegetable spray to grease a 12-cup Bundt cake pan.

In a large mixing bowl, mix together the flour, baking powder, salt, ginger, nutmeg, cinnamon, and cardamom.

Separate eggs in two bowls. Place yolks in a small bowl and whites in a large mixing bowl.

Beat the butter until smooth in another large bowl. Add the brown sugar mixing well after the addition. Beat in vanilla and continue beating for about 3 minutes.

Beat the yolks with a fork then add to sugar mixture. Scrape the sides of the bowl as you mix.

Add pumpkin puree to this mixture and beat until smooth. With a wooden spoon, add in the flour mixture. Beat only until dry ingredients are lightly blended.

Add cream of tartar to egg whites and beat until soft peaks form then fold whites into the pumpkin batter.

Spoon batter into prepared Bundt pan. Spread batter evenly around pan. Bake for 45 to 50 minutes. Allow the cake to cool in the pan for 10 minutes before removing then allow to completely cool. Dust with powdered sugar (if desired). Makes 20 servings.

Pumpkin Soup

Ingredients:

2 cups finely chopped onions

1/2 cup finely chopped celery

1 green chili pepper, seeds and veins removed, and finely chopped

1/2 cup vegetable oil

3 cans vegetable broth

2 cups fresh pumpkin puree or 1 16 oz. canned pumpkin

1 bay leaf

1-1/2 teaspoons ground cumin

1 cup evaporated skim milk

Parmesan cheese and fresh chopped parsley (if desired)

Instructions:

In a 6-quart saucepan, sauté onions, celery, and chili pepper in oil. Onions should be translucent, but not brown.

Add broth, pumpkin, bay leaf, and cumin. Bring to a boil. Reduce heat and simmer, uncovered for 20 minutes, stirring occasionally.

Remove bay leaf.

Add evaporated milk and cook over low heat 5 minutes. Do not boil. Add salt and black pepper, if desired.

Serve hot. Garnish with grated Parmesan cheese or chopped parsley. Makes 6 to 8 servings.

Toasted, Delicious Pumpkin Seeds

Ingredients:

1 1/2 cups pumpkin seeds

2 tablespoons melted butter

2 tablespoons sugar (or sweetener)

1 teaspoon salt (if you wish)
1 teaspoon fresh, grated ginger
1/2 teaspoon grated orange zest

Instructions:

Separate pumpkin seeds from the pulp. Sorry – there's no way around this. Separate the seeds from the pumpkin in water to make it easier.

Toss the clean seeds in a bowl with the melted butter, coating completely. Add seasonings and toss together.

Spray vegetable shortening across a cookie sheet and spread seeds in an even layer.

Bake for 30 minutes or until the seeds are golden brown. Stir the seeds once or twice as they are baking so that they toast evenly. Remove from oven and cool before saving in a tightly covered container. Serves 2-4 people

About the Authors

Joyce and Jim Lavene write award-winning, bestselling mystery and urban fantasy fiction as themselves, J.J. Cook, and Ellie Grant. Their first mystery novel, Last Dance, won the Master's Choice Award for best first mystery novel in 1999. Their romance, Flowers in the Night, was nominated for the Frankfurt Book Award in 2000.

They have written and published more than 70 novels for Harlequin, Penguin, Amazon, and Simon and Schuster that are sold worldwide. They have also published hundreds of non-fiction articles for national and regional publications. They live in Midland, North Carolina with their family and their rescue pets—Rudi, Stan Lee, and Quincy.

Visit them at:
www.joyceandjimlavene.com
www.facebook.com/joyceandjimlavene
http://amazon.com/author/jlavene
https://twitter.com/AuthorJLavene

Made in the USA
Middletown, DE
08 September 2021